S0-DTB-430

Career Year

A Major League Fable

by
Dan Briggs

authorHOUSE™

1663 LIBERTY DRIVE, SUITE 200
BLOOMINGTON, INDIANA 47403
(800) 839-8640
WWW.AUTHORHOUSE.COM

© 2005 Dan Briggs. All Rights Reserved.

No part of this book may be reproduced, stored in a retrieval system, or transmitted by any means without the written permission of the author.

First published by AuthorHouse 06/07/05

ISBN: 1-4208-6313-4 (e)
ISBN: 1-4208-4565-9 (sc)
ISBN: 1-4208-4566-7 (dj)

Printed in the United States of America
Bloomington, Indiana

This book is printed on acid-free paper.

I dedicate this book to the 2004 world champion Boston Red Sox. However, my lovely and talented wife, Mary Anne, told me I had to dedicate the book to her. Hmmm… decisions, decisions. Okay, how about both – thanks for the inspiration.

Also, thank you Mr. Joe Dillon and Dr. Tom Hill, who through their presentations, inspired me to improve my game.

Top of the 1st

Luke Kelly picked up the universal remote control and turned on his media center display — a fifty-two-inch, liquid crystal technology, wall-mounted unit with matching on-wall speakers. The display was the family room centerpiece. Luke scanned his favorite broadcast channels and selected the Professional Baseball Premium Network. From the game day listings, he chose the Red Sox versus Orioles game. The program informed him the game was in progress and asked if he wanted to continue. He entered "yes." Next, he was prompted which announcers: Red Sox, Orioles, or ball game sounds only. Luke chose Red Sox.

Luke was fifty-five years old with a lean body. He was clean-shaven and had a thin face. Luke was six feet tall with energetic blue eyes and short, thick, silver hair. He had a steady voice, and despite New England roots, he pronounced his R's.

"Reggie Cox steps up to the plate. Reggie is one for three today. He had a two-out single in the sixth," said the play-by-play announcer.

Wearing gray sweat pants, a loose-fitting blue T-shirt, and white athletic socks, Luke stood in the middle of the room holding the remote control in his hand.

"Reggie hits a come-backer to Torres. Torres looks off Sanchez at second and throws out Cox for out number two," said the announcer.

"Reggie was first-pitch hitting again. He needs to learn to be more patient in those situations. Something for him to work on," said the color commentator.

"Cripes, yes. Jeepers, Reggie, you've killed us all year by doing that with runners on," Luke groaned.

"Well it comes down to Nick Hudson with two outs in the Red Sox ninth. The Sox trailing Baltimore three to two. Hudson is oh-for-three, his average dropping to two thirty-eight. The Red Sox have only managed five hits off Baltimore pitching today. Torres delivers a strike. A good fastball catching the outside part of the plate. Hudson has a few words for home plate umpire Rich Boyer about that call," said the play-by-play announcer.

"Yeah, the pitch looked a little off the plate. Could be Boyer figures everyone just wants to go home," said the color commentator.

Luke rocked on his feet. "Rally spot, need to get into the rally spot."

"Torres eyes Sanchez at second. Doubt Sanchez is going anywhere, but the Orioles are being cautious. Sanchez has not stolen a base all season. The Orioles are guarding the lines. The pitch from Torres, a fastball inside and Hudson fouls it off his hands," said the play-by play announcer.

"It's gotten cooler as the day went on, that one might have stung. As you can see by the flags, the wind is blowing in, pretty breezy right now. Lots of papers and wrappers blowing around on the field," said the color commentator.

"C'mon, Nick, get a hit. Who cares about the weather? End the season on a good note," Luke said.

"Nothing and two count, two outs. Hudson trying to hang in there to keep it going. Torres looks in control with good stuff... And that will do it, Hudson strikes out swinging on a splitter in the dirt. The Red Sox lose the..."

Luke turned off the display center and tossed the remote control on the sofa. "Damn it, Dead Sox, what a pitiful season."

The video conference telephone rang in the study. Luke hustled from the family room into the adjacent study and answered the phone. The video data was blocked by the caller, allowing voice-only communications.

"It's always a pleasure to hear from you, John, so how can I help you?" Luke asked, standing next to his executive desk, which dominated the small room.

"Luke, on behalf of the group, I am checking with you again to ensure you are okay with proceeding," John said in a well-spoken, calm tone.

"Of course," replied Luke, "we have all reviewed this, and the consensus is for me to proceed."

"True. However, this project is definitely different than anything we have done before. The group was far from unanimous about going forward. It is not too late to make adjustments or select the alternative project. Let me remind you about your status. Please do not get me wrong, I love your confidence but -"

"John, this is important to me. It's important to the group. We all agreed about the benefits and potential results. I'm ready. I'm pumped up about this. It's how I need to feel in order to pull this off."

"I support you, Luke. Of course we want you to be successful, but things are going to have to fall into place for you to be effective. You know what the concerns are."

"This is a project that's worth the risk. The additional reports I requested will be available tomorrow, correct?"

"Yes, via a secure e-mail from me. Luke, you need to be successful, otherwise I am certain the group will terminate your participation. When you joined us, you knew our projects were challenges. And now you're about to launch a very difficult endeavor. As the group leader, I need to tell you that your peers are very concerned with your contributions. You are well-liked, but being well-liked is not why you are part of this group."

"The group can collectively kiss my butt when this goes down."

"Well, you know, I bet Hogan thinks you have a nice butt, so he may be okay with that."

"Hogan," Luke snickered. "Where did you find him? Hogan scares me. He doesn't want to kiss my ass, he wants to spank it."

"That would be an interesting sight. Maybe our next summit can start with that. I like to have plenty of interaction to kick off our meetings."

The Red Sox clubhouse at Fenway Park was active with conversations among players and coaches. Most were relieved the season was over. The manager and his coaches were certain to be fired. They were virtually fired months earlier by the New England sports media. The press relentlessly called for personnel changes when it was obvious the Red Sox were not a playoff contender.

Sitting in front of his locker, Red Sox third baseman Nick Hudson saw Pete Sullivan approaching him. Sullivan, a beat writer for the *Providence Herald* newspaper, covered the team. He dressed well, wearing fashionable casual clothes. Sullivan was thirty-eight years old and spoke with a nasally voice. Short compared to the athletes he regularly interviewed, he was five foot nine inches, medium build, with wavy, dark brown hair and wore wire-rim glasses.

"Nick, where do you think you will wind up next year? Do you think the Sox will re-sign you?" Sullivan asked.

"I hope to be right here in Boston, so I can spend more quality time with you, Sully," Nick said, not looking at the reporter.

"What are you going to do to improve your hitting and run production?"

Nick said nothing. He slowly stood up, turned, and directly faced Sullivan. Nick stepped toward the reporter. With arms at his sides and fists clenched, Nick towered over Sullivan. They stood inches apart. The clubhouse chatter diminished; locker neighbors watched the confrontation. Nick was six feet two inches, two hundred ten pounds, his athletic body complemented in a baseball uniform. The ballplayer's hazel eyes fixated on the reporter. Sullivan's eyes widened and his face turned red. The sports writer stood still and quiet.

"Wiffle ball," Nick said with a wry smile, and he stepped back.

"What? Wiffle ball?"

"Yeah, Wiffle ball. You know if you get some electrical tape and tape a Wiffle ball up a little, you can get some decent velocity and the thing really moves. If you can hit that, you can hit anything."

"Very intriguing, a true revelation, Nick. Do you want me to quote you on that one?"

"Sure, go ahead. But I know you're not going to quote me. You've got other quotes and stories here."

"Yeah, you're probably right."

"Mind if I share something with you?" Sullivan asked in a subtle tone. "You know we go back a bit, and it's the end of the season, and I -"

"You don't need an excuse, Sully. What's up?"

"This is hard to say, maybe you know already, but you are developing a rather difficult reputation. Don't get upset with me. It's things I'm hearing. I know you've had your personal setbacks in the past, but your actions -"

"You mean moodiness, inconsistent performance."

"Well, yes, exactly. Plus some of the comments you make. With no pun intended, you've made a few comments this year that were off the wall. You are so intense sometimes and other times easygoing. For God sakes, even just now I thought you were going to bite my head off and then you follow it up with something about Wiffle ball."

"If you need a quote from me, go with this: I will work on improving my intellectual consistency."

"The Red Sox and fans don't care about your intellect. How about on base percentage, slugging percentage, walk to strikeout ratio -"

"Thanks for the advice. Maybe you should apply for a hitting instructor position."

"No, I'm thinking about an invite to spring training. I can play third, you know. You should see me field a Wiffle ball." Sullivan smiled. He extended his arm and shook Nick's hand. The reporter walked away to continue his work.

Nick sat down, his mind and body exhausted from a 162-game schedule. He rested his elbows on his thighs; with shoulders slumped, he stared straight ahead. His short, brown hair disheveled. Nick's vision focused on the objects in his locker. The sounds in the clubhouse became white noise. The season and his brief Major League career played like a video. The highlights were not displayed. Nick viewed the mental and physical errors, strikeouts, and unlucky bounces. He heard the jeers from the fans. He recalled a strikeout in Detroit, a ground out double play against Chicago, a pop-up with the bases loaded versus Toronto, a poor swing on a ball in the dirt to end the season.

Bottom of the 1st

In the single-story country club home in the golfing community of Citrus Hills, Florida, Luke studied at his desk. A picture window framed the ninth tee. On a cool mid-December morning, the golfers were a steady parade. Luke scanned his reports, notes, and briefs while he listened to Johann Pachelbel's *Canon & Gigue.* He wrote several comments in his day planner. He synchronized his wristwatch with the computer's clock. Luke arranged papers and files, all dated, in chronological order, on the desk next to the keyboard.

"It's time," he said. Luke silenced the music and turned on the computer display's built-in video camera. Luke entered the required username, passwords, and fingerprint biometric credential to access the video conference. In a multiplexed view, he saw his fellow group members, each one a small picture on the monitor. With this meeting dedicated to Luke's project, he was the last one allowed to enter the conference.

"Welcome, Luke," John said in a booming voice. "Luke and others, you know the purpose of this meeting. I trust you have received and read the self-expiring, secure brief from Luke. Let me remind all of you, our focus this morning is Luke's project, and we have allotted forty-five minutes. Standard rules on confidentiality and security do apply."

"Let's get right into this," said a group member. "Have you made your final selection?"

"Yes," Luke replied. "It's the Hedgehog."

The group was silent.

"And is the Hedgehog on schedule for initial contact in January?" another asked.

"Yes, providing the Hedgehog is still around," said Luke.

"The Hedgehog had better be, Luke, or your plan will need serious work," a group member said sternly.

"There is such a significant risk with this project. I know we've debated this, but so many things could go wrong that Luke can do nothing to prevent. No matter how proactive he is, the whole project could be a waste. And speaking of waste, no offense Luke, but your record last year was dismal," voiced another peer. Several group members snickered.

"And are you sure Hedgehog is the right choice?" another asked.

Luke frowned and pointed his finger at the computer display. "First of all, last year is irrelevant. With respect to Hedgehog, our research is solid and confirmed by all of you. Damn it, c'mon everyone, what more do you want? Cripes, the results of this project could be huge."

"Luke, no need to defend or paint a rosy picture. Your colleagues' questions and concerns are valid. Let's discuss the hard facts and brutal truths, as always," said John, who was a stickler about group procedures and meeting protocol.

Luke nodded yes and took a deep breath. He realized his brief, emotional outburst was inappropriate.

"There are definite risks, as with any of our projects. This is a high-risk, high-reward type of project. I know this one has certain elements that stray from my control. However, even partial success could be beneficial. The Hedgehog's profile strongly indicates he is a capable and lifelong learner. The project phases have been well defined, increasing my chances for success. Total success can be realized even if the plan changes. The key will be how I spot those needs for change and react. That should ring familiar to all of us," Luke said. He saw two group members nod in approval.

The video conference continued with questions related to logistical issues associated with the project. Luke's answers were detailed. He referenced and recited from notes and files. Thirty minutes into the

7

questioning, Luke glanced at the computer's clock and his wristwatch. He was surprised how quickly the meeting had progressed.

"As per our guidelines, let's go around the horn for rapid response," John said. "Remember, your feedback to Luke should be short and to the point."

Luke listened intently to the advice and recommendations from his colleagues. He scribbled notes and comments into his notebook.

"So Luke, still into the healthy lifestyle? How are those protein shakes?" asked group member Hogan.

"Yes, Hogan, still drinking them every day. You know, you could have a nice ass too if you just worked at it."

The group laughed. Luke cracked a wide smile, showing his bright white teeth.

"Luke, any feedback for the group?" asked John.

"I truly appreciate your concern and input, including those who have different viewpoints regarding this project. As always, you inspire and challenge me."

"Thank you, Luke, we look forward to hearing more about your progress," John said. "One last thing, and I must be frank. I do not want to be a spirit buster, but Luke, you must achieve success on this project. Your colleagues and I have discussed this matter. If you fail, or measurable success is not recognized, we will terminate your participation in the group. Unfortunately, that would be a dubious distinction for you, the first person removed from the group for failing to achieve expected results. I have nothing more to add at this time, other than good luck. Peace be with you all, and I will talk with all of you soon."

Top of the 2nd

Driving his heavy duty Dodge Ram pickup truck, Nick Hudson exited the golf course parking lot. The late afternoon sun in Fort Myers, Florida shined brightly, so Nick grabbed his sunglasses from the center console. A blue Volvo sedan followed him.

Traffic was light on this Sunday afternoon. Listening to music on the Cruising Tunes radio channel and chomping on bubble gum, Nick drove leisurely. He thought about the golf round he just completed.

"Short game did it to me again," he said aloud.

Nick turned onto Tamiami Trail and he unconsciously increased his speed enjoying "Rockin' Down the Highway" by the Doobie Brothers. He paid no attention to the Volvo a couple car lengths behind him.

After driving ten minutes, Nick pulled into a parking lot. He adjusted his Nike golf cap, wearing the bill low, almost covering his eyes. The baseball player had a brawny face with a healthy complexion. During his rookie year in the major leagues, several coaches teased him about the local media stating he had movie star looks. The coaches dubbed him "Hunkster the Youngster."

Nick entered Hooters restaurant. The restaurant had a lively crowd, mostly men watching a football game while drinking beer and eating chicken wings. He sat at a table facing two plasma displays showing a National Football League playoff game.

The ballplayer pulled a golf scorecard from his shorts pocket. He reviewed his round. He tracked strokes, greens in regulation, and putts.

Sitting alone, Nick noticed a man approaching the table, staring straight at him. The man walked with purpose. He wore a long-sleeve white dress shirt, solid navy blue tie, and khaki pants.

"Hi Nick, I'm Luke Kelly. Could we talk for a few minutes?" Luke extended his hand.

"Hi, nice to meet you. Do you want my autograph or something?"

"Autograph?" Luke snickered. "No, I was hoping we could talk." Luke sat at the table, directly across from Nick.

"Listen buddy, I don't mean to be rude, but I am waiting on someone, so —"

"Hi, guys. Can I get you something to drink?" said the Hooters waitress. She leaned over the table to pick up a wrapper, showing off her busty figure.

"Can we have a few minutes, please?" replied Luke. The waitress smiled, nodded yes, and walked away. "So how's your baseball career going?" Luke asked.

Nick sighed. "Great. You know -"

"That answer's as fake as what was just hanging over our table."

The two men briefly stared at each other.

Nick chuckled. "Okay, dude, what do you want to talk about?"

"I want to help you. By the way, my name's Luke."

"Help me? And just how can you help me?"

"You have to commit to letting me help you."

"And I want to do this because?"

"I know your Major League performance is struggling. You are capable of so much more."

"Hey man, I don't need -"

"You hit two thirty-eight last year, two forty-five the year before, and only thirteen home runs over that time period. Also, you have an on-base percentage well below the league average. Not exactly the hitter the Red Sox thought they were getting when they drafted you seven years ago."

"That's great, dude, all information you can get from the back of my friggin' baseball card. Anything else you want?" said Nick, agitated with the uninvited visitor.

"I also know your father died of ALS while you were in high school. Your younger brother was killed by a drunk driver when you were at the University of Maine."

Nick's eyes widened and he scowled. "Listen, asshole, I don't appreciate you bringing that up. It's time for you to leave," Nick said, raising his head and chest.

Luke stood up and pulled a business card from his shirt pocket. He placed the card on the table. Printed in bold, black text was the word "PCing." There was no address, Web site, or person's name on the card.

"PCing, what's that?" Nick asked.

"Personal coaching. Turn over the card for the way to reach me. I highly recommend you do."

Nick turned over the card. The card read, "When the student is ready, the teacher will appear." Underneath the phrase was a handwritten telephone number.

"And when you call me, you'll need to enter a personal identification number. And that you could get from looking at your baseball card. You're a smart guy. I am sure you will figure it out."

Luke walked away from the table and left the restaurant. Nick did not watch him leave. He held the card in his right hand and re-read the statement, "When the student is ready, the teacher will appear."

"Who was that guy?" Nick said aloud.

The day after Nick's encounter with the stranger at Hooters, he joined his teammate on the golf course. The two ballplayers enjoyed their regular January golf outings.

"Nice shot, Rooster," said Nick to Rooster Colby. Rooster was a lanky twenty-eight-year-old with shaggy, dirty blond hair, a weak growing goatee, and tobacco-stained teeth. He was a speedster, contact hitter, and the league's best lead-off man. The Red Sox centerfielder was tagged with his nickname because he crowed like a rooster with animated facial contortions, while sitting on the bench. He crowed for no apparent reason other than to get a laugh from his teammates. One time, at a game in Seattle, with a lively performance by Rooster, the police officer working the visitors' dugout approached a Red Sox coach. The officer pointed over his shoulder toward Rooster, and whispered to the coach, "Tourette's?"

"No," replied the coach, "Gamecock."

The two athletes strolled from the second hole tee box to their golf cart.

"Have you ever heard of PCing?" asked Nick.

"PCing? No, dude, what do they play?" replied Rooster with his South Carolina drawl.

"No, it's not a music group. It stands for personal coaching."

"Nope, never heard of them. Why do you ask?"

"Yesterday, this older guy comes up to me at Hooters and says he wants to help me." Nick pulled the PCing card from his shorts pocket and showed it to Rooster. "He gave me this business card."

"There's no name on the card."

"Yeah, the guy said his name was Luke."

Rooster and Nick hopped in the golf cart, both men silent. Rooster drove the cart to his ball. Each man grabbed an iron from his respective golf bag and continued playing. After finishing the second hole and walking off the green, Rooster turned to Nick.

"You know, he could be a shrink hired by the Red Sox," said Rooster.

Nick stopped walking. "That's an interesting possibility. A shrink? We know they hire motivational speakers. You'd think if they wanted me to work with a sports psychologist, they'd talk to me first about that. Just spring on it me, that's strange."

"Yep, I've heard they do that, not just the Red Sox either. But hell, I'm not sure how I even heard about it."

"Yeah, so how do I find out? I mean I can't call the new skip and ask him. Imagine how that would go over. 'Hey, Skip, I was wondering, did the ball club hire a shrink for me, because I'm a friggin' nut case you know.'"

"You could call your agent."

"No, I don't think that would be a smart move from a business perspective."

"So just call the guy then and find out. Shit, if nothin' else, the shrink could help your putting."

Nick sneered at Rooster's comment regarding his putting. As they rode together in the golf cart to the third hole tee box, Nick considered his friend's advice.

"Yeah, I guess I'll call the guy. I feel fortunate to have gotten the one-year deal. If they're doing this, I shouldn't screw it up. If he's legit -"

"Hey, there's the beer girl. C'mon dude, let's get a couple of beers."

"Ah yes, the beer girl hottie. The only reason you play this course."

"Damn straight, Hudster. What is it about beer girls at golf courses? I swear they all look damn good. You know somebody ought to come out with a beer girl golf calendar."

"Okay Rooster, I'll call *Playboy* and *Golf Digest* and get right on it, so long as you stop crowing in my backswing."

Nick played the rest of the golf round without mentioning PCing or Luke. But his curiosity about Luke swelled after he left the course. "Who was that guy and why does he want to help me?" he repeatedly asked himself.

The fourth floor apartment balcony, with modest outdoor furniture, faced the intercoastal waterway. The apartment's interior decorations were college dorm room motif. A forty-eight-inch flat screen media display center, leather sofa, and virtual reality gaming chair dominated the home. Towels, batting gloves, wrist bands, baseball caps, hand weights, athletic bags, and clothes littered the living room floor.

Nick sat in a patio chair and gazed at the early evening sky. The twenty-nine-year-old bachelor twirled a smart phone in his hand. His Topps baseball card and PCing business card lay next to each other on a round table. Nick reflected upon his baseball career. Thoughts drifted to his deceased father and brother, and why the stranger at Hooters mentioned them.

He slowly dialed the telephone number written on the business card. He put the phone to his ear and heard two ring tones.

"Hello, thank you for calling. Using your keypad device, please enter your personal identification number," said the automated female voice.

"Personal identification number, from my baseball card? Let's see, date of birth." Nick entered six digits.

"Sorry, that is an invalid number. Good-bye." The call disconnected.

"Screw you. Okay, how 'bout the baseball card number, four, eight, nine." Nick dialed again, entered the three digits, and received the same result.

"Damn it. Now I'm going to get this thing." He surveyed the baseball card front and back. The card pictured the right-handed hitter in the batter's box swinging at a ball from the third base dugout view.

"I got it. My number, thirty-seven." He dialed again and entered three seven when prompted.

"Number accepted," said the automated response. "Please hold while your call is connected."

"Yes!" Nick said, pumping his fist.

"Hello, student, thank you for your call. At the tone, please leave a message including your telephone number and I will call you back promptly," said the voice mail greeting from Luke.

"Voice mail? Shit." Nick pulled the phone away from his ear. "Oh, what the hell." At the tone, he said, "Yeah, this is Nick Hudson, give me a call. My number is..."

Bottom of the 2nd

He followed the guidelines from his colleagues, sending the initial call to voice mail. Be careful not to seem overanxious, make the student demonstrate desire, do not rush what is important, and balance urgency with natural progression — were recommendations from the group. Luke was bursting with excitement from Nick's call. He reminded himself to think and move slowly.

Luke sat at a desk in his hotel room, with the curtains open, allowing him to watch the sunrise. He reviewed notes and the project file on his laptop. As he had done years ago for sales calls, Luke practiced his lines and voice mannerisms. He lectured to himself, "The response has to be genuine, enthusiastic, and to the point." Using his laptop and microphone headset, Luke dialed Nick's smart phone number.

The phone rang, waking Nick from a sound sleep. Nick stretched his left arm from the bed and grabbed the phone on the nightstand.

"Hello," he mumbled.

"Good morning, Nick, this is Luke Kelly. Thanks for calling me."

"What?" replied Nick in a groggy voice, lying in his king size bed covered with pillows, blankets, and clothes. He glanced at the clock radio on the nightstand. "It's friggin' six in the morning."

"Yes, and it's important we get started early, that's why I'm calling you now. Let's get together this morning at nine. Your golf club will do nicely. I know that would be convenient for you and a safe place for us to talk."

Nick sat up. "Dude, I sure hope you're not a scam artist or something."

"Trust me, I want to help you."

"Okay, see you at nine. Any chance we're playing golf?"

"Sorry, Nick, not today. I'll meet you in the Sable Palm conference room at the club."

Luke wore gray dress slacks, polished black leather shoes, a light blue dress shirt, and navy blue blazer. He knew blue shirts and jackets made his azure eyes look brighter. At a table facing the door, he sat alone in the small conference room and sipped ice water. Luke checked the time on his wristwatch. It was ten minutes after nine o'clock. Sitting and standing, standing and sitting, he stretched his neck and shoulder muscles. He grabbed his smart phone from the table and put it back down. For five minutes, Luke paced.

"Nine fifteen, where is he?" Luke said aloud. He stopped pacing and inspected an aerial photograph hanging on the wall. His back was to the door.

"So did the Red Sox hire you?" asked Nick, standing inside the doorway. Luke spun around.

"Well, hello Nick, I'm glad you're here," Luke said, standing on the opposite end of the room.

"Are you going to answer my question?" replied Nick. He sported black cargo shorts, white ankle socks, golf shoes, a maroon mock-neck golf shirt, and his favorite golf cap. Luke strode across the room and greeted Nick with a firm handshake.

"Thanks for meeting with me." Luke motioned toward the table. "No, the Red Sox did not hire me. Sit down and let's talk. I'll explain."

Luke closed the conference room door. He joined Nick at the table, sitting straight and attentive.

"I'm giving you five minutes. Who the hell are you?" Nick asked in an aggressive tone.

Luke smiled. "I've had business presentations that started out with the same intro. I like your get-to-the- point style."

"My guess is you're a shrink, right?"

"No, I am not a psychiatrist. Do you need one?"

"No, what I need is a long-term contract. Got one of those?"

"I think I can help with that. Interested?"

"Can we dispense with the verbal dancing? You're running out of time to tell me why I should be here."

Luke recalled the feedback and concerns from the group. He would be dealing with a different breed. A profession no one in the group can relate to. A lifestyle foreign to anything the group's collective knowledge and experience could understand.

"The fact that you called me and showed up today says a lot," said Luke.

"Don't put too much into that. To be honest, I think the team is involved."

"First things first, let me tell you about PCing."

"Good. I did some research on the Internet and through search engines. I didn't find a damn thing on PCing, and the amount data on personal coaching was friggin' overwhelming."

"PCing does not have a Web site. I do not have any brochures, pamphlets, or electronic media. PCing is not a business. There are no contracts or any sort of paper trail with the students. We are —"

"So how much are the Red Sox paying you?"

"The Red Sox did not hire me."

Nick snickered. "Oh, now I get it. How much are you going to cost me, Mr. Personal Coach?"

"That depends upon —"

"What an interesting business. Seek out professional athletes, do some background information on them, and try to scam them for some bucks." Nick stood up and placed both fists on the table, flexing his tan, defined forearms. "Hey dude, screw you, I don't need your help."

Luke remained visibly calm, although his heart rate accelerated and he felt flush. He quickened the pace.

"You didn't let me finish my last statement. I was going to say it depends upon you. My services cost you nothing. You decide what to pay, if anything at all. It's totally up to you. Like I said, there's no written contract or agreement. I don't want one. I also want this to stay confidential. All of the projects are like that."

"Projects?"

"Yes, projects. I have helped people make a major difference. Much of it depends upon what I call 'clap.'"

"Clap? What's that, the venereal disease coaching method?"

"Clap, it stands for cooperate, listen, apply, persist. But if your VD reference helps you remember the process, that's fine."

Both men chuckled. Nick pulled a chair away from the table and sat down.

"Do you remember taking a written test just after coming back from the All-Star break last season?" asked Luke.

Nick glanced upward and rubbed his chin. "Yeah. The whole team did. A lot of weird questions, I remember."

"It was a combination IQ and emotional quotient test. You not only did well, you scored among the highest in all of Major League Baseball, which includes coaches and managers too."

"Among the highest, huh?" Nick snickered. "Damn, why couldn't they pay bonuses for that? I thought the test was something being used by the team to evaluate our ability to solve problems."

"That's what was told to the league and players union."

Luke reached into his blazer breast pocket and placed a half-folded document on the table.

"Recognize this? That's your completed test."

Nick's eyes widened. He stared at the document for several seconds.

"So let me get this straight, you created this test and got the league to do it?"

"Not quite. A colleague of mine hired a company who hired a company to arrange for the testing. It was a good deal for the teams, but I'm fairly confident they did very little with the results."

Nick examined the test papers, inspecting the handwriting and signature.

"Okay, this is all very interesting, but who are you?" Nick said, pointing his finger at Luke.

"There will be plenty of time for you to get to know me better. I'm more concerned, and you should be too, with getting started and moving in the right direction. We have a lot of work to do."

"Did you play Major League ball?"

"No, and I am not a technical coach. You're surrounded by a plethora of talent who can help you technically. I will be coaching you in other ways."

"So you can't help me hit a slider? What good are you?" Nick said, cracking his first wide grin since they met.

"If you work with me, apply what you're taught, and persist, you'll be hitting sliders and just about every other pitch."

Nick leaned back and ran his hands over his golf cap. He sighed deeply and glared at the test document.

"Okay, so what are you asking me to do? What's next?"

"There are three rules I need to explain." Luke stood up and walked to a flip chart. "First rule is confidentiality."

He wrote the word *confidential* on the flip chart in all capital letters using a black marker.

"Who have you told about me or PCing?"

"Just my teammate Rooster Colby."

"That's it?"

"Yeah, what's the big deal? Why does this need to be confidential?"

"Your success needs to be all about you. And it will be, but we can't have your teammates, coaches, the media, and whoever else questioning or interfering with us. It would turn into a mess. In order for you and I to achieve success, this needs to be kept quiet. Please do not mention me to anyone. Okay?"

"Yeah, no problem. I'm sure Rooster will forget about it, so don't worry."

"Fine. The next rule is security." Luke wrote the word *security* on the flip chart in the same manner.

"You know, you're pretty good with that flip chart. Shit, you've even got neat handwriting," Nick said with a smirk.

"Yeah well, years of practice. I remember my employees called me White Board Luke. Supposedly I couldn't communicate with anyone without using a white board."

"That's okay. I've had a few coaches like that too."

"Anyway, only call me on the number I gave you and you must use your personal identification number. If I suspect the phone number or personal identification code has been compromised, I'll need to change it."

"Oh yeah, the personal identification number, very clever, dude."

"Last rule is commitment. You must commit to the program. I know you've heard that kind of thing before. I admit, I'll ask you to do some different things, so I need you to work with me. Trust me."

"Dude, trust is earned."

Luke smiled. "Great point. Fair enough. Work with me and let's watch the trust unfold. It will be fun."

"Yeah, you look like a real fun guy," Nick said sarcastically.

"All right then, I will see you this evening at five o'clock at the Publix on Cleveland Avenue. It's the one not too far from here."

"Tonight? We're meeting at Publix, the grocery store?"

"That's right, see how fun I am," Luke quipped.

Nick drove his black pickup truck into the supermarket parking lot. Luke, wearing beige dress shorts with a brown leather belt and light blue golf shirt, waved to Nick, acknowledging him. Luke stood next to an outdoor round concrete picnic table near the front entrance to the store. Luke watched Nick approach and muttered, "I sure hope this student is ready."

"Are we going to get some food?" Nick asked with slight grin.

"We sure are. But first, we have a few things to go over."

Luke propped his right foot on a concrete bench next to the table. "You know, Nick, there isn't anything complicated about this. The programs are quite easy to grasp. It's the discipline and execution that trips people up."

Nick listened, blocking out traffic and the bag boys rounding up shopping carts.

20

"Half the equation is purely physical."

Luke pulled a blue chalk stick from his shorts pocket and drew a line down the center of the table.

"Kind of like a relationship with a woman. This is getting more interesting," Nick said.

Luke continued without hesitation. On the left side of the table, he wrote "50%".

"If you nail down the physical aspects, your chances for success grow tremendously. No matter what profession, the best performers are physically fit. Sure, there are a few exceptions, but without question, if you feel great and are healthy, you are halfway there."

"Dude, no kidding. I'm a professional athlete, and I consider myself in good shape."

"Good shape? You are satisfied with good shape? How about great shape? *Dude,*" Luke said mockingly, "you are a professional athlete, which relatively speaking makes the physical dimension actually more difficult to achieve."

"Hey, I agree, but I've got access to some of the best trainers and training programs on the planet. What are you going to offer me?"

"Great question. My program, or recommendation, is very simple." Luke wrote "CLEAN FUEL."

"Now we can go shopping. Let's go," Luke said.

Nick rolled his eyes. He pointed to the table. "Hey, what's the other half of the equation?"

"There are two other pieces. We'll get to those later. You have a long way to go, Grasshopper."

"Grasshopper? What are you talking about?"

"Never mind, let's go."

The supermarket was bustling with customers. January was a busy time; year-round citizens combined with snowbirds and tourists increased the Fort Myers population.

"Here Nick, you drive," Luke said, motioning to the shopping cart.

"You know, you can call me Hudster. That's what guys on the team call me. I prefer that."

"Ballplayers and nicknames, I wonder why that's so prevalent."

"Dude, that's just the way it is."

"And calling me dude, isn't that rather immature?"

"Okay, Mr. Luke, sir."

"That sounds like crap. You can stick with dude."

In the furthest right-hand aisle, the two men walked next to each other with Nick pushing the cart.

"So take a guy like Ed Chimelewski, the relief pitcher, what do you call him?" asked Luke.

"That's easy. Chewy. I mean, you can't say Chimelewski. By the time you say 'C'mon Chimelewski, throw strikes,' the inning is friggin' over. And try saying Chimelewski with a wad of tobacco or gum in your mouth. As a general rule, we have to stick to one or two syllables only."

"Why not Eddie?"

"Eddie? That's what his mother would call him. If the nickname is something that your mother would be okay calling you, it's not gonna work."

"Hmmm, sounds like a very complex and advanced culture."

Nick slowed the cart, scanning the aisle. "Dude, there are a lot of good-looking women in here."

"Haven't done a lot of grocery shopping, have you? Well Hudster, from what I can see, most of them are checking me out."

Nick laughed. "Please, no pun intended, but you are out of your league."

"Okay, watch the next few women who pass by, guarantee more will smile and say hi to me than you."

"You're on, old man."

Their walk shifted to a strut. The two well-built men, both dressed in summer golf attire, carried their heads higher. Two elderly ladies nearby ignored them. An attractive woman with light brown hair, in her thirties, and professionally dressed in a blue pinstriped pant suit meandered close.

Nick and Luke both made eye contact with her. She looked away and then glanced at Luke. The woman acknowledged him with a slight smile and said hello. When the encounter passed, Luke chuckled and Nick shook his head in disbelief.

"Well, aren't you just the babe magnet," Nick said. "Shit, you probably take Viagra."

Luke smirked and stared straight ahead.

"You do! You take Viagra, don't you?"

"There's nothing wrong with Viagra. It's a good product. But -"

"You stud. Viagra Taker... VT, yeah, there's your nickname. If you played ball, we'd call you VT."

"Okay that's enough, we need to get back to business. Turn the cart around. We need to head over to produce."

"So VT, where are you from?"

"I live in Citrus Hills, Florida."

"I've heard of it, where is it?"

"North of Tampa and southwest of Ocala."

"You married?"

"I was. My wife died six and a half years ago."

"Sorry to hear that, man." Nick stopped the cart in the produce section. Luke continued on, a couple feet ahead. "Tell me, the other day at Hooters, why did you bring up my father and brother?"

Luke turned and faced Nick.

"I'm sorry I did that. It was out of line. I had to make a point that I knew about your background. I would like to learn more about you, your goals, your dreams, what you want to accomplish as a professional."

"Seems like we both have had some serious crap occur in our lives, huh?"

"Life isn't life without enduring serious crap."

"Let me write that one down. I could use that quote next season with the press."

Luke grabbed two bunches of bananas. "You'll be eating a lot of these."

"Is that what you mean by clean fuel? I've had all kinds of information thrown at me about nutrition. I know the subject matter well."

"Yes, but do you follow it? Don't even bother to answer, I already know. You're in good shape, hell you ought to be, plus you're only twenty-nine."

Luke placed two fresh strawberry pints into the cart, along with several apples. "Okay, a few more items and we'll be done. Help me find the flaxseed oil."

"Flaxseed oil?"

"Oh yeah, you're going to love flaxseed oil."

The two men returned to the same concrete table after putting the groceries in Nick's truck. With the table between them, they faced each other. Luke scribbled in earnest his key points on the table.

"Just friggin' protein shakes?" Nick asked.

"Don't forget the raw almonds, sunflower seeds, and water," Luke replied. "And you need to start tomorrow."

"You've got to be joking. You want me to go the entire season eating... drinking practically nothing but protein shakes. You're nuts, better yet, you're friggin' almonds."

"Do you want to have a high-performing body? You must have clean fuel. You've got to stop eating garbage."

"You have no idea what it's like playing pro ball, do you? Shit, I've seen guys throw shutouts totally hung over."

"Remember the commitment rule? I told you I would ask you to do some different things. But I admit, your work environment does present a challenge. So I've got three golden rules regarding your diet."

With the blue chalk, Luke scrawled "FINES."

"Every time you break training in a given week, you must pay me five hundred dollars."

"Five hundred dollars!"

"Yes, you'll think twice about cheating if you have to pay a hefty fine. You're human, you'll fail at some point, but the fines will keep it to a minimum. Rule number two," Luke said, and he scribbled "CHOCOLATE MILK."

"After an intense workout, I want you to drink chocolate milk. Two glasses, no more, and you must use one percent milkfat or skim milk. Don't chug it. I want your post-exercise drink to include protein and carbohydrates. The chocolate milk will provide that, plus it tastes good. And chocolate has some unique benefits for the brain. Chocolate contains a neurotransmitter called serotonin that acts as an anti-depressant. Some other substances in chocolate have a stimulating effect. So combining an intense workout followed by chocolate gives your brain and body a nice double whammy. You could even ask the team's trainer about this, if you have a concern."

"Ah yes, the power of Ovaltine."

"And rule three," Luke stressed, and he jotted "PRE-BEER WATER."

"Chances are you'll be drinking beers with your teammates, especially on road trips. If you do, and I hope you do not, I want you to order and drink a large glass of ice water before you start drinking the beer. Hopefully, this will help you only drink two or three beers instead of five or six or more. Your teammates won't notice and they'll think you're just doing good to keep yourself hydrated by drinking the water. Which you must do. Oh, and another thing, make it light beer."

"You're serious, aren't you?"

"I'm telling you, you've got to treat your body like a finely tuned racing car, a machine that requires clean fuel. The program won't start out easy, but the good habits will develop. This diet may seem extreme, but it's not. Our bodies crave this diet if we train ourselves correctly. Nutrition and supplements are critical to performance, regardless of one's profession. If you were, say, a business executive, I'd still have you eating right. A protein shake for breakfast every morning, and you'd eat healthy eleven out of the fourteen remaining meals for the week. I'd give the business exec three treat meals per week, no more. If the business executive has more than three treat meals, the fines kick in."

"How come I don't get any treat meals?"

"Think about it, Nick, c'mon."

"Hey, you're not pushing ephedra or creatine or steroids are you? I can't do that shit."

"Of course not. Your protein shakes will consist of quality whey protein, fruit, water or lowfat milk, and the flaxseed oil."

"Dude, how about a steak every now and then?"

"For five hundred bucks, make it a good one."

Nick's smart phone rang.

"It's my agent, I should take this," Nick said.

Nick walked away from Luke. He spoke in a hushed tone for less than a minute. Luke did not hear the conversation, nor did he try. Nick approached the table smiling.

"Good news?" Luke asked.

"Yeah, it might be. The Phillies signed Lopez. The Sox were considering him. Looks like I have the inside track on the third base job. Hey, maybe you're a good luck charm."

"I'd like to think so. Successful people do consider themselves lucky." Luke tapped the table with the blue chalk. "Okay, back to work. A couple other things, you will be receiving a list of good foods and bad foods. Stay away from the bad foods. If it's not on the good list, assume it's bad. And remember this one, stay grounded when flying. In other words, no drinking alcohol on the plane. The only thing you shall drink on a plane is bottled water."

"You're into details, aren't you? You remind me of my ninth grade math teacher. A real pain in the –"

Luke clapped his hands together once. "Cooperate, listen, apply, persist," he said sternly.

"You are such a quack. How the hell did I get stuck with you?"

"Another thing," Luke said, "your body gives you very definitive feedback every day regarding the quality of your diet. You need to be having clean floaties."

"Clean what?"

"Your shit should float and you shouldn't have to wipe your ass."

Nick said nothing and stared at Luke for several seconds.

"Haven't you learned this?" asked Luke.

"Excuse me, but no, I didn't major in crapology at Maine. My God, you give new meaning to the word *anal*."

"That's the nicest thing you've said to me since we met. I'll call you tomorrow morning and let you know where to meet."

Top of the 3rd

Two elderly men sat monitoring their fishing poles planted in shallow water. A crescent moon was visible in the clear morning sky. Luke sat with his legs crossed on the compacted sand, facing the ocean, and admired the rhythmic waves. Several joggers and walkers streamed by. Luke sensed someone approaching from behind.

"Damn, you always get somewhere early," Nick said.

The two men greeted each other. They strolled along the beach, engaging in small talk. Luke carried a foot-long wooden dowel.

"So why me?" asked Nick. "There are about seven hundred major leaguers for you to choose from."

"I was wondering when you were going to ask."

"Is it because of how I did on that test?"

"That's part of it. A software program was developed to help determine which players would make the best students. Things like age, education, contract status, big versus small market team, everyday player versus pitcher, and several other factors were all analyzed. Imagine my surprise when a player from my favorite team was among the top three candidates."

"You're a Red Sox fan?"

"Borderline neurotic, yet intelligent fanatic would be a more accurate description."

"Have you coached any other ballplayers or athletes?"

"No, this is a first for me."

"Great. Can you tell me some people you have coached?"

"I can't divulge names or get too specific. My area of concentration is working with entrepreneurs. I proposed this project and got approval to proceed... barely."

"You used the word 'project' again. What's up with that? Is that what I am to you?"

"I have to say, you're listening. I like that. I'm an up-front guy, so I'll tell it like it is."

The two men stopped walking and faced each other.

"PCing helps people who can make a difference. Yes, every coach deeply cares about his or her student. And at the same time, the coach expects the student to make a major impact. That's one reason we refer to each student as a project. But there is another reason. One thing we all agree upon at PCing is happy people have a project. In other words, look at a successful person and you will find he or she is involved, online, and into something that makes a profound and positive impact in his or her environment."

Nick gazed at the ocean waves. "You trying to go deep on me, dude?"

"Let me put it another way: You have a huge opportunity to be influential. You need to execute, and if you do, based upon what I have learned about you, you can achieve wonderful things, and really be a player, so to speak."

"So tell me, who have you worked with recently? Not names, just give me an idea."

"Hmmm... you know about the space elevator being built? PCing coached a person who was key to making that happen. And we worked with a leading nano-technologist to help develop and market more effective solar panels. But that's just a couple of projects out of hundreds."

"Were you coaching those guys?"

"Not those specific projects. Last year I worked with a businessperson regarding, let's call it a pig manure processing venture. It didn't work out as PCing had expected. I still have hope, though."

"Between me and pig manure, you've had some real shitty projects, huh?"

Luke laughed. "I love what I do with PCing. I just hope I can continue."

"How many people are part of PCing?"

"There are twelve of us and a leader."

"So how did you -"

"That's enough about me, let's focus on you."

With the wooden dowel, Luke bent over and etched a circle in the wet sand. "Remember when I said yesterday there were two other pieces to the equation?"

"Yeah."

Luke drew lines, creating a one-half and two quarter sections. "The next part is intellectual." In the upper quarter section, he wrote a capital I.

"This is an area you could really excel in," said Luke. "There are three things I want you to do."

In the sand, Luke wrote "BRAIN BURN."

"First, get a hold of the team's video director and get him to print you a picture of you hitting the heck out of the ball. The picture must be one of you in great form. I mean one you're really proud of."

"And what do you want me to do with it?" Nick asked with a puzzled expression.

"Make about six or seven copies; you may need various sizes. Then, I want you to post those pictures in key places, preferably in a spot that forces your eyes to move up and to the right. For example, definitely put one on your bathroom mirror, upper right hand corner. On your refrigerator, well, maybe next to your blender since you'll be making all those protein shakes. In your locker for sure, and put one in your wallet so that you see it every time you open it up. One in your truck too, near the dashboard."

"Aside from people thinking I'm an egomaniac, what am I accomplishing here?"

"You're going to burn that image into your brain. Your brain will help your body support that form. This isn't anything revolutionary or new, but it works, so you should do it. A PCing colleague told me how this really helped a doctor who had to do some public speaking, but was petrified to do it. She got a picture of a similar looking woman, standing on stage, confident, focused, with the audience paying close attention. She thought about that picture when she had to give a presentation. It's how she pictured herself, and when she did speak, sure enough, that's what she looked like."

"Yeah, that's a real nice story, but the hell with the team's video guy, I'm gonna talk to my golf pro about this."

"Just do what I ask."

"Okay, that's number one, what's the second thing?" Nick asked. With his bare feet, Nick pushed the sand back and forth. Luke noticed he appeared like a hitter, smoothing out a batter's box.

Luke scribed "BAROQUE MUSIC."

"When you watch video of opposing pitchers, I want you to do so while listening to baroque music."

"You mean classical music?"

"Not just any classical music, but specifically baroque music. I'll get you the music. Just make sure you watch plenty of video this season while listening to baroque music. This music will help you focus. No need for me to get into too much detail. You can research this topic yourself. The music generates creativity and makes those brainwaves hum."

"And I just love it when those brainwaves are humming," Nick replied with a broad grin.

"Third one." Luke wrote "READ." "You need to read a book per week."

"A book per week? I don't read a book a year."

"That's disappointing. A smart guy like you. What do you read?"

"I like magazines. *Sports Illustrated, Men's Journal, Newsweek, Golf Digest,* stuff like that."

"Wow, a real renaissance man. Well, that's going to change. You'll be getting a reading list from me. Follow it closely. The magazines are fine, but starting next week, you'll be reading one book per week.

31

You'll like the reading, and the books I've picked out will help your performance."

"What the hell? A book per week? No way. My schedule's not going to allow that."

"Nonsense. A half hour per day. All that time you spend on planes. Cut out one TV show per day, and you've got it. Besides, most of the books I am assigning you are relatively short. Don't worry, *War and Peace* isn't on the list."

"Damn, you're going to turn me into a nerd. Shit, what's next? Are you going to have me reading Shakespeare in the dugout? Between the baroque music and the reading, my teammates will think I've lost it. And how the hell is reading books going to help me hit better?"

"The goal is to improve your total intellectual performance. I hear all the time how important the mental aspect of the game is, especially hitting. You're a professional, and anyone who considers themselves a professional must be constantly learning, and improving their intellectual abilities. Your physical skills, with respect to your peers, are probably average, so you need to get your edge from other areas. Don't sell short the things I am asking you to do. They will make you a better person."

Nick peered at the smoothed sand for several seconds. "You know, that's funny. I joked with a reporter last season that I would improve my intellect. I had no idea that I would actually do it."

"Not only intellect, we need to get into the third piece. This will require a road trip. I'll make the travel arrangements and will call you later today with the details."

"Road trip? Where are we going?"

"You'll find out soon enough."

Bottom of the 3rd

Nick stood on the sidewalk outside the baggage area at the Phoenix International Airport; his carry-on duffle bag lying next to him. Rent-a-car buses and taxis rolled by. Loud noises from pile drivers and construction vehicles were constant from the parking garage being built across the street. Nick scanned the roadway, waiting for his ride. Unshaven, wearing sunglasses, blue jeans, gray sweatshirt, and a faded University of Maine baseball cap, he chewed gum and checked his smart phone for messages.

An elderly man hunched over and hobbling with a cane approached Nick. Nick glanced at the man and turned his eyes away.

"Excuse me," said the old man in a Mexican accent - barely discernable. He did not look up at Nick, unable to lift his head. The slow-moving elder spoke to Nick's brown Wolverine boots. "Could you give me five dollars for a taxi ride? I need five more dollars for the fare."

The old man wore a tattered poncho and a large straw hat which covered his face. Nick noticed his right hand shook as he held the cane.

"Sure, dude," Nick said. He opened his wallet and gave him a ten-dollar bill. "Here you go." Nick put the money in the old man's left hand, which was cupped upward.

In one seamless motion, the old man dropped the cane, pushed off his hat, and stood up straight. "Atta boy Nick!" exclaimed Luke.

"Luke, what the hell are you doing?"

33

Luke patted Nick on the shoulder. "Just an attitude check. You passed. Although I'd be more impressed if you gave me the twenty. Let's go, I'm parked over there." He stuffed the ten-dollar bill into his pants pocket.

"Damn, you've got to be one of the weirdest dudes I've ever met."

Luke picked up his props and marched toward the parking lot. "Hold on, Nick, it might get weirder if you're lucky."

"Hey, I want my ten dollars back."

It was the kind of drive that allowed for meaningful conversation. The traffic was light, highway driving, and clear, dry weather. The trip from Phoenix traveling north on Interstate 17 provided picturesque yet monotonous views. A perfect backdrop for individuals to engage in enjoyable dialogue. Luke knew the drive well. He loved the southwestern United States. He and his wife made the trek many times before. Friends teased Luke about his southwestern vacations, saying he simply sat on a rock for several days.

"Let me guess, we're going to the Grand Canyon," said Nick, positioned in the passenger seat of the hybrid economy rental car.

"No, that certainly is a great place, but we are going somewhere I consider very special."

"Where?"

"It's not just where, but it's how we get there and what we will do."

"Whatever, as long as it doesn't involve drugs or getting naked."

"Absolutely no drugs. If you want to get naked, that's up to you." Luke scanned the landscape. "Beautiful country, isn't it."

"Yeah, if you like brown," Nick replied.

"So tell me, how's a good-looking young man such as yourself not married?" Luke asked.

Nick stared at the desert terrain. "I guess I had my opportunities. Things just never worked out. I was practically married to a girl in college, but once I graduated and went to play minor league ball, things broke off."

"What about all those baseball groupies I hear about?"

"Oh yeah, they exist big time. But you have to be real careful. I've had some fun, but nothing serious ever materialized."

"That doesn't surprise me."

Nick turned his head toward Luke. "What do you mean?"

"Nothing negative, actually it's a compliment. I could tell from your profile, you know, the test you took, that you are very sophisticated. You just suppress it. Or better said, you do not cultivate it."

"What does that have to do with getting hitched?"

"I think it means you won't settle. You have a very strong instinct about right and wrong. You recognize that marriage is more than just a physical attraction."

"You are a friggin' shrink, aren't you?"

The drive continued, escalating, and getting cooler. Luke brought raw almonds, apples, and bottled water to eat and drink.

"So here I am out in the middle of nowhere with you, which I can't believe I'm doing. We're traveling in what amounts to a lawn mower with doors, and I know there's nice golf courses in Phoenix, so I'm pissed that we're not playing golf, and -"

"What's your point, Nick?"

"My point is, what's your friggin' angle? What do you want from me?"

"It's simple. I want you to be incredibly successful. You don't even realize it, but you are in a unique position to have major impact. Remember, I need you to cooperate, listen, apply, and persist."

"Yeah the clap, I understand, but -"

"For the last hundred years or so, our society has experienced a mixture, or call it a collision, of economics, social conditions, technology, a zest for entertainment, and somewhat warped values that has created both opportunity and imbalance. What if we could seize more of the opportunity and improve the balance? That's where you can make a difference."

"Listen, Emerson, according to the world I live in, I'm an all-glove, no-hit infielder, just trying to stay in the big leagues."

Luke chuckled.

"What? What's so damn funny about that?"

"I'm impressed that you're familiar with Ralph Waldo Emerson."

"Yeah, well don't tell anyone. I had to write a report about him in college. VT, you just concentrate on driving."

Luke gathered backpacks and clothing from the trunk of the car. Nick stood next to the vehicle and observed Luke meticulously prepare the backpacks.

"Here," said Luke and he tossed Nick a black thirty-two-ounce Louisville Slugger baseball bat.

"What's the bat for?"

"For right now, it's a walking stick, and when you don't need it, attach it to your pack. It will come in handy on the way down when you're sliding on your butt."

"We're going to hike to the top of that rock?"

"Yes, the views are awesome." Luke recognized concern in Nick's question. "Haven't done much hiking or climbing, have you?"

"My idea of hiking is playing a round of golf without a cart. You know, I'm sure my contract has some crap in it about me not doing this kind of stuff."

"This is cake. It's a trail, for crying out loud. There's actually very little climbing involved. And the way the trail is, if you do fall, it will only be a few feet. Jeepers, don't be a wuss."

"Screw you, let's go. Don't make me kick your ass."

Luke was excited about the one-and-a-half-mile round trip hike. He had brought two backpacks, bottled water, gloves, two flashlights, and a lightweight jacket for Nick, which was needed for the forty-five-degree temperature. Luke soaked in the environment. The brilliant blue sky provided a striking contrast to Sedona's most famous red monolith - Cathedral Rock. The sense Luke appreciated the most was the sounds. Natural and unpolluted, a needed change from his norm. Something he had to experience at least yearly. During his business career, Luke had developed several methods to re-energize his mind, body, and spirit - Red Rock Country provided a supercharge.

The two men began their ascent. Nick carried his Luke-issued baseball bat. Luke held a valued hiking pole, a gift from his wife years ago.

"Tell me, is this some exercise to improve my self-esteem? Is that what you're into?" Nick asked.

"Self-esteem? I'm not working with you just to improve your self-esteem," Luke responded sharply.

"Hey, I touched a nerve there."

"There's healthy debate about this, but I believe it's performance that improves self-esteem, not the other way around. An improvement to performance brings self-esteem along for the ride. Haven't you noticed the things I've asked you to do are all practical? Nothing mumbo jumbo about it. I want you to achieve peak performance. You could have low self-esteem and still perform well. Too much self-esteem can be a bad thing; it inhibits the learning process. Like so many things, balance is important."

"Okay Doc, I was just asking a question."

Luke chuckled. "Yeah, I guess that was a mini rant wasn't it?"

The pair hiked up the trail at a comfortable pace. Luke was in no hurry. This was a short trip to his favorite Southwest destination. The hike was secondary to what he wanted to accomplish at Cathedral Rock this afternoon.

"Hey, so what did you do before PCing?"

"Lots of things, you could say. I had my own sound company in Weymouth, Mass. We worked Boston and the surrounding areas."

"Sound company as in what?"

"Sound systems for schools, churches, businesses, and home theatre systems."

"How did you get into that business?"

"Well, I went to Berklee in Boston, got my degree in business, and then started from scratch with a dream and a credit card."

"You went to a music school and majored in business?"

"Yes, and I played a musical instrument also."

"What did you play?"

"Electric guitar."

"No way. Mister Anal played electric guitar? That would make you somewhat cool."

"And I don't mind saying, I'm pretty good too."

"Why didn't you do something playing the guitar?"

"I had my gigs, but I realized I had a passion for business and wanted to build something."

"So what happened to your business?"

"I sold it and moved on."

"Moved on to PCing?"

"No, there were other things I did prior to PCing."

Both men enjoyed the scenery as their hike ascended. The moderate climbing was no challenge for either man. Nick stopped occasionally to experience the views and would catch up to Luke.

"So what do we do when we get to the top?" Nick asked.

"What do you do when you hit a home run?"

"Circle the bases."

"Before you do that."

Nick smiled. "Enjoy it."

And enjoy it they did. Both men moved slowly, making three hundred sixty degree turns to absorb the colorful surroundings.

Luke took off his backpack and placed it on the red rock. He inhaled deeply and raised his eyes skyward. "Standing next to God."

"What do you mean?" Nick asked.

"That's what this feels like to me."

"A religious man?"

"Yes, although perhaps more spiritual than religious. What about you?"

"I think it's safe to say there's a lot of praying in baseball."

"Nice answer, but I'm not letting you off the hook. What about you?"

Nick sighed. "I'm not a religious fanatic or anything. I mean I'm not in church once a week. I'm not a Bible reader. But I do believe in God. Although there's been a few times I've been very pissed at Him."

"Pissed because of what happened with your family?"

Nick gazed at the distant east side of Sedona from the one thousand foot perch above the desert floor. "My father really suffered the last few months. It was tough for everybody, especially my mother. You know, you think of your dad as old, especially when you're sixteen. It wasn't until after college I truly realized my dad died at a very young age, thirty-nine. Damn, I've got teammates that age."

Nick turned toward Luke and stared at him. "When Larry died, that was just awful. I was away from home. I wasn't going to go back to Maine, but my mother convinced me it was the right thing to do. I still think of Larry often. He probably would have been the better ballplayer, such talent."

"Tell me, have your family tragedies affected your ability to perform?"

Nick raised his eyebrows with a perplexed expression. "You know, nobody has ever asked it that way. They always ask how has it affected my performance. I have to say, those things affected me in many ways, but I've always felt like it doesn't have anything to do with how I perform. At the pro level, you have to own your performance regardless of what happens or what has happened."

"So, what do you need to do to play better?"

"You said something about an edge," Nick grinned. "That's a pretty good term as we both stand up here. And that's what I need, and to be honest, that's the main reason I decided to work with you. Desperate times call for desperate measures."

"Desperate for what?" Luke sat down next to his backpack.

Nick paused. "Success."

"And what's success?"

Nick took off his backpack and sat a few feet opposite Luke.

"It's so many things. A respectable batting average, all-star performance, World Series ring, a multimillion-dollar contract."

"And what if you had those things?"

"I'd be happy."

"And what would that do for you?"

"Isn't that what everybody wants?"

"Sure, but the things you mentioned, will they always keep you happy?"

"They would if I achieved them every year."

"Oh, really? All-star every year, World Series ring every year, millions of dollars every year. Anyone ever done that, for say, twenty years?"

"No, of course not."

"What are the best things you like about playing baseball?"

"It's a beautiful thing to make nice plays and I love to make perfect contact with the ball. Solid hits are sweet."

"Yeah, but couldn't you get those experiences from playing in a recreational softball league?"

"It wouldn't be the same. The whole MLB experience is awesome. The best stadiums, the best players, the competition, my teammates, the fans, the biggest friggin' baseball stage in the world."

"So in a way, it's the total environment that makes an impact on you? And impact is important? Such an outstanding environment and experience that you're desperate to work with an old fart like me in order to stay in the big leagues. Is that fair to say?"

"Well... yeah, especially the old fart part."

They sat on the red spire and talked for another hour. Luke philosophized about human evolution, and ranted the human species was destined toward sure extinction unless there were significant changes. Nick discussed the lifestyle differences between major and minor league baseball. No one else joined them.

With the sun setting, the bright orange glow produced both striking and complementary colors in the sky and on the spires - another visual experience for nature's show at Cathedral Rock.

"Before we head back down, put this iPod on," Luke said. "I've mixed together a soulful collection of music that you will enjoy. And while you're listening, I want you to swing the bat I gave you."

"What for?"

"Trust me. You will remember this forever, Mister Ballplayer. The sights, the music, swinging the bat on top of this rock. Just do it."

Nick stood up and adjusted the headset to hear the music. He held the bat with both hands. Nick glanced at Luke and the bat.

"Got pine tar?"

"Swing the bat," mouthed Luke.

Nick shrugged his shoulders and took a half-hearted golf swing.

"Swing the damn bat!" shouted Luke, his voice carrying over the peaks of Cathedral Rock and into Red Rock Crossing.

Nick was taken aback by Luke's outburst. The right-handed hitter gripped the bat and rhythmically moved his fingers, tightening his grip. He moved his feet into a slightly closed batting stance, glared out toward a make-believe pitching mound, and swung the bat.

"Keep swinging, Nick!" shouted Luke. He walked away, sat down, and stared into the sunset sky.

The music was a collection of rhythm and blues, hard rock, and soul. Nick swung the bat with power, putting his entire body into each swing. He blasted hits all over the imaginary field surrounding Cathedral Rock.

When the music stopped, Nick dropped the bat next to his backpack and took off the headset. Luke approached Nick, his face sweating from the twelve-minute exercise.

"Okay, what the hell was that about?" Nick asked.

"Anytime I can combine moving music, the beauty of nature, and a part of one's professional skill, it always provides positive energy, especially here."

"No offense, seems like mumbo jumbo to me. What did you do for the pig manure guy? Did you have him lug a pig up here and shout 'Shit, pig, shit' while playing 'Old MacDonald Had a Farm'?"

"All I can say is, you will remember this forever. And while it may seem absurd, I bet you felt good, probably still do. Never underestimate the power of a vortex."

"A vortex?"

"Yes. I have some literature. You can read about it."

"Great. Just what I wanted to do tonight."

Nick and Luke sat at a table in a clubhouse restaurant at an exclusive resort, a thirty-minute drive from Cathedral Rock. The casual dining room was quiet; only two other tables were occupied. They relaxed at a four-person table next to a large window. The view overlooked lighted tennis and croquet courts adjacent to a mountainous red rock.

"Hey, are we getting dinner? I'm starved," said Nick.

"Yes. I've arranged for that."

"This is a nice place. You must have some money."

"I did all right for myself."

"A lotta money in sound?"

"The business did well. I was lucky."

"So what did you like best about your business?" asked Nick, imitating Luke's broadcaster quality voice.

"God and Bach."

"Huh?"

"God and Bach is a sound industry phrase that has to do with designing and installing sound systems for churches and synagogues. For us techies, it's a challenge, and rewarding, to deliver a system that sounds perfect for speech and music. My business didn't make a lot of money in churches, but my fondest memories are those systems and how well they worked."

A waiter carrying a tray approached the table. Nick glanced at the waiter and back at Luke.

"Gentlemen, here's your order," said the young waiter. He placed two bowls of raw almonds on the table, two large glasses and a white porcelain pitcher.

"What's this?" Nick asked.

"Dinner," said Luke.

Nick threw both hands up into the air. "Shit, we're having protein shakes?"

"Yes, what did you expect?"

Nick chuckled. "Well, now that I think about, this is exactly what I would expect from you." Nick grabbed the pitcher and poured the vanilla banana shake into his glass. He lifted the glass toward Luke and clinked the other glass on the table. "Peace, love, save the whales," Nick said and took a full swig.

During their meal, the conversation centered on baseball and Nick's journey to the big leagues. Nick talked about his all-state performance at Narragansett High School, and despite his father's ailing health, how well he played. Nick had the opportunity to play ball at a private school and perennial baseball power in Providence, but his father was adamant about playing for the local school. For two consecutive years, he was Rhode Island's best high school shortstop and hitter. "I could count on things going right on a baseball field," he told Luke.

Nick reminisced about his stellar play at the University of Maine. Maine converted him to a third baseman, where he realized he was better suited. "But it wasn't so much how I played at Maine that got me drafted as it was how I played in the Cape Cod League. My play in the Cape Cod League got me noticed."

"Would you say that Major League ball is your toughest challenge yet?" Luke asked.

"No shit. You ever stand in the box and face ninety-five mile per hour heat?"

Luke leaned back and grinned. "Okay, hot shot, you ever have to meet payroll when cash flow sucks?"

Nick responded quickly, "You ever deal with the constant scrutiny of the Boston sports media?"

"You ever have to deal with an audit by the Department of Labor?"

"You ever go for an oh-for-sixteen slump?"

"You ever deal with slumping sales while being on the hook for a nut considerably larger than your salary?"

"You ever deal with half a season of traveling?"

"You ever experience expense reports that are totally out of control? And by the way, while you may travel a lot, at least it's with teammates. Imagine the poor schmuck who travels all the time by himself."

"As a rookie, you ever get dragged to a strip club by a few veteran teammates and they make you dance on the table for dollar bills?"

Luke paused and stroked his chin. "Okay, that is pretty bad."

Both men laughed. They were silent for a few minutes as they drank their protein shakes.

"So you fly me out here and haven't told me the third piece," Nick said.

"Thanks for asking." Luke patted his chest, feeling for a pen.

"Need something to write with? If I made you explain something without writing it out, I think you'd go into convulsions."

"Yeah, very funny. You have a pen?"

"Nope. I sense you're about to get tremors."

Luke scanned the table. He picked up the porcelain pitcher and poured a circle on the green tablecloth.

"Stop it! Damn it, Luke. Yo, waiter, excuse me. You have a pen and paper for my friend?"

Satisfied with a pen and cocktail napkin, Luke drew a circle.

"Yeah, I got the circle. Just get into the third part. I assume it spells pie. What does the E stand for?"

"Emotional."

"And what three things do I need to do to improve my emotional intelligence?"

"Well, I guess you're catching on."

"C'mon, this isn't hard."

"You're right, it isn't, but most people don't have the discipline to do the things I am asking you to do. So with that in mind, I would say it's very hard, next to impossible for some. And it's not emotional intelligence, it's emotional balance."

"Okay, fine, but I'm off to a good start. I've been doing the protein shake thing. You're not getting any five hundred dollar fines from me yet.

And other than today for our little journey, my off-season workouts are going great. You're not even aware of that. So, just keep it coming."

Luke smiled and nodded with approval. He placed the napkin squarely on the table and wrote "GET AN NBA."

"Do you mean MBA or NBA?"

"NBA, as in no-brainer activity."

"Shit, I've got plenty of those."

"You might, but you really need to focus on doing a single NBA everyday, or at least close to it."

"What exactly is an NBA?"

"It's a cardio-respiratory activity that doesn't involve much thinking about the activity, but allows you to do a lot of thinking. If that makes sense."

"Sure, you mean things like jogging, walking."

"Yes, but you need to do them alone and for at least thirty minutes every day. And it doesn't have to be intense from an exercise standpoint. It's the thinking that matters."

"That's cool. What are the benefits?"

"Huge benefits. Relieve stress, creative thinking, sorting out problems. Your best thoughts will occur while doing your NBA. And here's the other key part about your NBA. At the conclusion of it, you should determine one thing you are going to take action on. It could be to research something, follow up, add or modify something you are working on. Remember, tell yourself to take action on one thing after doing the thirty minutes of quality thinking. Write it down if you need to."

"What is your NBA?"

"Actually, I have two. I love to run and the other I call heavy-handed shooting."

"You're scaring me. I'm not sure I like the sound of that. What the hell is heavy-handed shooting?"

"I shoot baskets in my driveway wearing weighted gloves. I do plenty of lay-ups, jumping, and constant movement, not just knocking down free throws."

"Damn, VT, you actually sounded athletic there. How old are you?"

"Biologically or chronologically speaking?"

"I didn't know I had a choice. It was a pretty simple question."

"My chronological age is fifty-five, but my biological age is thirty-eight."

"Must be those protein shakes that make you feel so young," Nick said in a sarcastic tone.

"It's my lifestyle. Change your lifestyle for the positive and you can have optimal performance. Gee, I bet that sounds pretty appealing to a young athlete," replied Luke with a smirk.

"Okay, what's the second thing here?" asked Nick and he tapped his finger on the napkin.

Luke penned "SITUATION SILENCE".

"I think many good athletes do this, but chances are, only on game day, so to speak. I want you to practice situation silence everyday. It's a powerful exercise if done correctly and consistently."

"What is it?"

"For thirty minutes, I want you to lie down on your back, be still, and be quiet. No music, no TV, no games, no distractions. Let your mind and body relax. Relax all your muscles, including your neck, shoulders, and jaw. Tell yourself your legs and arms are heavy. Become physically and mentally comfortable, slow your heart rate down, let your mind recharge. You will begin to feel at ease. This exercise will allow you to picture your personal success. Every day you should envision how you will be successful. And soon you'll look forward to this daily exercise."

"You know, I've suddenly got a lot of thirty-minute exercises. Reading, an NBA, and now this."

"Let me tell you why I call it situation silence. How long is a situation comedy? You got it, thirty minutes. Eliminate watching one television show per day, just one, and you'll have the time. By the way, doing situation silence when you first wake up in the morning or before you go to bed at night doesn't count."

"Such a stickler for proper execution," Nick wisecracked.

"Let me add that many great performers were often considered aloof. I think it's because of NBA or situation silence, or both. These people knew they needed this recharge, a time to be alone. If you haven't been doing this, it could explain your inconsistency at your craft."

"This is great, when I get asked what I did to make the All-Star team this year, I'll tell the press I attribute it to daily thirty-minute naps."

"It's not a nap, it's -"

"Certainly pitchers will fear me if they know I've had my power nap. I can hear the opposing team now, 'Pitch around him. He's had his nap and he watched you on tape while listening to baroque music, which only strengthened his nap, so -'"

"Nick, Nick."

"Yeah."

"Screw you."

Nick laughed. "Don't worry, I may just do this shit. You're anal as hell, but you're a good guy. C'mon, tell me the third thing about emotional balance."

"Before we get there, there is another important step with situation silence. Right after completing it, you need to write down a key word, phrase, or couple of sentences about something you thought about which would help you be more successful. This must be recorded in a journal and each entry dated so you can look back on what you thought and wrote. You can record in a notebook or laptop, whatever works for you. Keep it brief. After thirty or more entries, you'll be amazed how creative you are."

"I'll be amazed if I do it thirty or more times." Nick saw the disappointment on Luke's face. "I'm kidding, listen-"

Luke stood up. "Excuse me, I need to use the restroom." Luke walked away from the table and left the clubhouse dining room.

Nick doodled on the paper napkin, watched college basketball highlights on his smart phone, and scanned the near-empty restaurant several times. Ten minutes passed.

"He must be taking a clean floatie," Nick joked to himself.

"Sir, the gentleman you were with asked me to give you this," said the waiter, and he handed Nick a letter-sized envelope.

Nick opened the envelope and read the one-page note.

"Nick, I have a business matter to tend to. Your room is set up, just check in at the front desk. Your bag is in your room. Tomorrow morning at eight, a limo will pick you up and take you to the airport. The limo driver will have your flight details. Also, in the limo will be a package containing your reading list, an iPod with baroque music (largo movements), good foods and bad foods list, and a Web site that has excellent protein shakes recipes. Enjoy! After our conversation today, I know just the place to discuss the third part to emotional balance. I will call you tomorrow evening."

The letter was signed "VT."

"Sir, is everything all right?" asked the waiter.

"All right? Forty-two friggin' dollars for protein shakes and almonds?" Nick asked, holding the check.

"Custom order, sir."

Top of the 4th

"You must be Hudson," said the burly maintenance worker in a gruff voice.

"Yes," replied Nick.

"I been waitin' on you for about a half hour," he grumbled. "But I don't mind, time-and-a-half, you know."

The maintenance man grabbed the identification badge clipped to his shirt pocket and held the badge to the proximity card reader. The door unlocked and he pulled it open.

"Here you go, you know the way. I unlocked the other doors. The guy you're meetin' is on the infield, been here about a friggin' hour. You ballplayers keep some weird hours."

Nick walked down the dimly lit corridor leading to the clubhouse. The clubhouse was vacant. Cardboard boxes, benches, chairs, tables, and paint buckets were scattered about from renovation work. Nick weaved his way to the first base dugout. He spotted Luke sitting on third base, gazing at the clear, midnight sky. The stadium lights were off, stands empty. Only the faint glow from the new Jumbotron scoreboard behind the centerfield fence provided light.

"This your idea of mood lighting?" Nick joked.

"Thanks for coming."

"Who do you know at the City of Fort Myers to arrange this?"

"I've got my connections," Luke said in a coy tone. "How was the trip back? Did you get the package with the stuff?"

"Yeah, I got the stuff. So did you tend to your business matter?"

"Yes, I suddenly remembered I had a conference call I had to be on. Plus, I need to keep you on your toes."

"You planned the whole damn trip that way. I know your type. You don't take a shit without a game plan."

Luke scanned the field. "This year's spring training is critical to your success."

"Tell me you didn't bring me out here in the middle of the night to tell me that."

"You know, I've heard and read your bat has potential."

"As I've heard several times, potential is a minor league term."

Luke faced Nick and took a deep breath. "Nick, all winning teams need heroes. Players, if you will, who make a difference, because they can, and because they care. Like politics and economics, heroism has more impact with the people and activities that surround us. Regardless of one's profession, superlative performance can lead to direct and indirect benefits. Players are needed who take their beliefs, combine them with their unique talents, and produce tangible and immediate results. I think you're that kind of person."

Nick crossed his arms and stared at Luke for several seconds. "Any chance you're a voting member for the league's Most Valuable Player award? Because if you are, I'm certain I've got one first-place vote."

Nick's sarcastic comment was remedial to the teacher. Luke recalled when his operations manager at the sound system business counseled him about entering into profound discussions with the employees. The operations manager told him, "Luke, these guys' idea of philosophy is talking about the Patriots' play calling on Monday morning. They're only debating this philosophical stuff with you to watch you get riled up. It's become the unofficial office spectator sport."

"So are you going to explain the third part to emotional balance or not?" Nick said sharply, interrupting Luke's thoughts.

Luke walked away. He stepped onto the pitcher's mound, bent down, and picked up a small keyboard lying next to the rubber. He faced the Jumbotron scoreboard.

"I just love this stuff," Luke said.

He pressed enter on the keyboard. Immediately, the scoreboard displayed the words PRACTICAL PRAYER in red capital letters, filling the scoreboard screen. The lighted words illuminated the centerfield grass with a red glow.

"This oughta be good," Nick mused.

Nick lounged on the grass adjacent to the pitcher's mound on the third base side. "You know, I'm a little disappointed with your special effects. I would expect trumpets to blare when you brought up practical prayer. I mean, you're a sound guy, c'mon."

"You have to pay extra for that."

Luke took a seat on the grass next to the mound on the first base side.

"When you pray, who do you pray to?" Luke asked.

"Are you asking me personally or is that a rhetorical question?"

"Prayer is our communications with God. It's a very powerful, emotional, and personal activity. And if the Holy Spirit lives within all of us, we are in essence communicating with ourselves through God. Therefore, the need for practical prayer."

"Okay, Father Luke, what is it?"

"Praying for world peace, an end to cancer and world hunger is all well and good. But practical prayer is different. It's more personal and can change our lives. Let me give you a simple example. Say a college student has a test the next day in physics. She is really stressed out about it. She has struggled in the class and the subject matter is tough. So she prays to God that she will perform well on the test. Deep and intense prayer. What do you think about that?"

"Why doesn't she stop praying and start studying?"

"Exactly. When we want to accomplish something, something realistic and obtainable which would help ourselves or others, but it's a challenge, we need to engage in practical prayer."

"Hey, let me guess, this a thirty-minute daily activity."

"No. It could be as long or short as you like. The key is reflecting about what you are trying to achieve and then asking yourself and God if you have done everything you could to make it happen. If the answer is no, then ask yourself what else you could do to succeed. Practical prayer pushes you to action, not hope."

"So what do you want me to do? Drop to my knees before getting into the batter's box and practically pray I get a hit?"

"That would be an interesting sight, and would be better than the spitting and the cup adjusting you guys do all the time."

"Okay, I hear you, but in my line of work I'm always up against someone. A pitcher and a team who are directly trying to stop me from being successful. And God cares about them too."

"All the more reason for practical prayer. Your profession is not alone. Businesspeople and lawyers are constantly competing. I bet the most successful ones do practical prayer, whether they realize it or not. I'm not talking about getting on your knees or going to a house of worship. If that's what you need to do for practical prayer, that's fine. I'm talking about having a two-way conversation with God that forces you to be creative and persistent with addressing problems, challenges, and opportunities where you have a real stake in the outcome."

"And what if in my two-way conversation with God, I don't like the answers?"

"Chances are, you won't. Practical prayer gets you to work harder, apologize, be more considerate, get involved, check your ego at the door, and do things others don't have the courage to do. I'm talking about intense dialogue here. You have to work at making prayer have impact. Just like I have to work at my guitar playing and you need to work on hitting. If you act upon what you're told through the Holy Spirit, you'll like the results and will be happier with yourself."

"Do I practically pray the Red Sox win the World Series?"

"No, the fans pray the Red Sox win the World Series. You engage in practical prayer to make you do the things to contribute toward winning a championship. If you're being honest with yourself and God, you will realize what you can control and impact. Then you have to execute."

Luke stood up and entered a command on the keyboard, turning off the scoreboard display. "It's time to call it a night." Luke walked onto the pitcher's mound and Nick joined him.

"So is that it?" asked Nick.

"That depends; it's up to you."

"What's next?"

"You've done a nice job of cooperating and listening, and I need you to continue doing that. But I also expect you to apply and persist. This is what I would like next. We should meet or talk on the phone every week for about -"

"A half hour."

Luke smiled. "Yes. But call me anytime, you know how to reach me." Luke and Nick shook hands.

Nick stepped off the mound and Luke patted him on the back. The ballplayer reached the first base dugout, turned and saw Luke walking across the third base coach's box.

"Hey Luke!" shouted Nick. "May the force be with you!"

Luke spun around. "Like I haven't heard that one a thousand times," he muttered. Luke hollered back, "Nick, I've got the force! I'm working to make you one!"

Bottom of the 4th

Crack!

"That's such a beautiful sound, isn't it, Rooster," said Nick. Nick and Rooster stood behind the batting cage at the Red Sox spring training facility watching their power hitting teammate take batting practice.

Rooster remained focused on the hitter. Both men leaned their arms on the cage railing. Rooster chewed tobacco, spitting every few seconds.

"A golf ball hitting the bottom of the cup, a basketball swishing through the net, a bowling ball crashing the pins for a strike. Those are cool sounds," Nick said.

"Yep," replied Rooster, and he spat.

Rooster and Nick stared at their teammate as he launched ball after ball into the late morning sky.

"So how was the fantasy camp you did?" asked Nick.

"It was okay," Rooster said and he snickered.

"What? What happened?"

"Oh nothin' really."

The ballplayers were silent for a minute, observing their teammate's hitting.

"You know, every time I help out with one of those things, it reminds me how lucky I am. I mean, there's dudes there payin' thousands of dollars, doin' something I get paid millions of dollars to do. You know what I'm sayin', it's kinda strange. And the other thing, some of those guys really suck. But they don't care, their havin' fun," Rooster said.

The slugger's batting practice continued for several pitches with neither man saying anything to each other.

"Rooster, you remember taking that weird written test last year after the break?"

Rooster thought about the question. "Yeah."

"Did you ever find out how you did?"

"Nope. Hell, I just connected the dots."

"Connected the dots? It was mostly short answer and fill-in-the-blank."

"I connected the dots anyway."

Nick continued watching his teammate's impressive hitting exhibition. He stared at the centerfield scoreboard for several seconds.

"You ever heard of baroque music?" Nick asked in a low voice.

"What? Broken music? What's that?"

"No, not broken music. Baroque music, it's classical."

"Nope. Humanities class was a long time ago, dude."

Nick nodded in agreement. He watched several balls fly over the centerfield fence.

"You familiar with Ayn Rand?" asked Nick.

"The country singer. Yeah, she's hot."

"No, she's not a country singer. She was a novelist and philosopher."

Rooster turned his head toward Nick.

"Novelist and philosopher!" Rooster exclaimed with tobacco and spit spewing from his mouth. "What the hell are you puttin' in those damn protein shakes?"

"I'm just -"

"Let me tell you somethin', Hudster. Don't be a tweener."

"A tweener?"

"Yeah, a tweener. Make a choice between bein' an idiot or a smart guy, but don't be in between, a tweener. Look, anything in baseball that's in between sucks. You try to field the in-between hop, you boot it, make an error. You get into a rundown, you're in between bases. An in-between swing is like a check swing. You can't get hits makin' check swings. Shit,

Hudster, anybody who talks to you for a few minutes can realize you're a smart guy. Damn it, be a smart guy, that's who you are. But commit to it and don't be pussyfootin' around about it. Our team needs smart guys and idiots. Be yourself, I guarantee you'll friggin' hit better."

Rooster adjusted and tightened his batting gloves.

"Get outta there, Hambone!" yelled Rooster to his teammate. "It's time for this so-called Punch 'n' Judy hitter to get his rips."

Nick grinned. He felt a rush of enthusiasm and relief, as if he just tapped an internal energy source.

"Don't be a tweener. I bet Luke would like to hear about that one," he thought.

Sitting in a lawn chair, Luke gazed at the printed name and words. He whispered, while classical piano music softly played from the iPod he clutched in his hand. His words rambled.

"I'm not sure if he is ready. Perhaps this project is a mistake. Six to six with a tiebreaker, far from a mandate. I don't know, perhaps my participation in PCing was a mistake. He has the skill sets. I need him to use them. I really do want to stay with PCing. Yes, this is important to me. Helping others. You know I've always wanted to make a difference, have impact. At this point, I need him to produce."

Luke paused. He reached to the ground and repositioned a rose-colored vase so it was centered.

"And this weather is one reason I moved to Florida," he mumbled to the tombstone, his breath visible in the chilly southern New England air. Luke turned off the portable music player and tucked it into his coat pocket. He folded up the lawn chair. As he walked away from the grave, Luke observed a black four-door sedan parked behind his vehicle on the narrow paved road in the cemetery. Luke walked slowly through the graveyard while watching the suspicious car.

Two men, wearing dark trench coats, exited the front seat and stood next to Luke's vehicle. Luke strained to identify the men. From one hundred yards away, he immediately recognized them. Luke quickened his pace and approached them.

"Hey, what a pleasant surprise. What are you guys doing here?" Luke asked.

"First Thursday of every month. You're so predictable," said John McFarlin, the PCing leader.

"That and our GPS works real well," said Bill Hogan, a PCing colleague.

"Jeepers, I forget about our GPS. Good thing I'm living a clean life, otherwise I'd get kicked out. Well, maybe it won't matter." Luke dropped the lawn chair and hugged each friend.

"You could have picked nicer weather, you know," said Hogan. "Thank God I've got this coffee. You realize there's a Dunkin Donuts coffee shop about every hundred feet up here."

"I bet that's loaded with cream and sugar," Luke said, looking at the large, steaming cup Hogan held in his hand.

"Yeah, Luke, what's your point?"

Hogan was a fifty-four–year-old stout man with black thinning hair. The PCing colleagues teased him about having an uncanny resemblance to the boss character in the *Dilbert* cartoon strip. Hogan spoke in a raspy voice and his tone expressed confidence.

"Gentlemen, we're not here to discuss the weather, coffee, or Hogan's excessive sugar intake," said John. The PCing elder was seventy-five years old, six feet three inches tall, with bushy eyebrows and a thin, wrinkled face. If he were to sport a beard and don a top hat, John could pass for Abraham Lincoln. A few in the group called him Honest Abe.

"So why are you here?" Luke asked.

"We thought we would check up on you and see how you are doing. It's important to remember that we need to guard the guardians," John said.

"I'm here only because President Lincoln offered to buy lunch," joked Hogan.

"The regular season starts in a few weeks. How is your student doing?" John asked.

"So far, I'm pleased. We talk at least once a week, and interestingly enough, he's very engaging in conversation about the books he's reading."

"I must say, Luke, I was always impressed with your lesson plan for this project. The physical, intellectual, emotional pieces for success. Simple, but I like it," said Hogan.

"Yeah, we'll see how it unfolds over the course of the season," replied Luke.

"Regardless of how that young man does in baseball this season, the lessons taught and insight shared will serve him well. Immediate results are not always realized, but you know our ways," John said.

"Yes, PCing has made it very clear."

"You know I support you. I recruited you; of course I want you to succeed. You started out so well and then two projects that failed to produce. We had to -"

"Three strikes and you're out," Hogan interrupted with a grin.

"Thanks for the ironic analogy," Luke said.

"Luke, no matter what happens, you're my idol. Look at you, fifty-something and your body looks like a twenty-five-year-old. Good God, if I had that physique, my wife couldn't handle me," Hogan said.

Luke raised his eyebrows at Hogan. "You could do something about that."

"What? Are you kidding? I do have to work at this figure. It's a perfect image for dealing with all those Washington bureaucrats," Hogan wisecracked.

"Gentlemen, let's sit down together somewhere, talk, and have lunch. Luke, you choose the place. I'll ride with you, and Hogan can follow. I also want to discuss our upcoming summit in Savannah."

The PCing leader extended his hand and touched Luke's shoulder. "Although I never met your wife, I am sure she was a wonderful person."

John paused. "So, your project, how do you feel about its progress? I'm still satisfied with my decision to support it. Sure would like you to –"

"John, thanks. I'm pleased to say the student is doing well. The first phase of my project is complete and I would define it as successful. At this point, it's basically time to... play ball."

Top of the 5th

Tired and hurting, Luke relaxed in the hotel bed. Aches and soreness reminded him of his accomplishment. The throbbing in his left knee was a different matter. Luke stared out the hotel room window, entranced by the evening's April rain. He glimpsed at the clock radio on the nightstand.

"Jeepers, it's six fifteen, I'm missing *Sports Center*," he said to no one. Luke grabbed the remote control and searched through the on-screen menu. He found the channel and pressed enter.

"...ah yes, the struggles of Heartbreak Hill, the thrill of finishing and the agony of da feet," said the *Sports Center* broadcaster. "Over twenty-two thousand runners participated in America's oldest annual marathon today, with hundreds of thousands lining the streets and cheering..."

"That's me! That's me!"

He jumped from the bed and grimaced in pain when his left leg hit the floor.

"I made *Sports Center*! I was on *Sports Center*! I'm a *Sports Center* highlight!"

He looked around the dimly lit hotel room, unsure what to do next. He lunged for his smart phone and stubbed his toe on the nightstand.

"Jeepers! That friggin' hurts!"

Luke pressed the speed dial function and caller identification blocking command, while hopping on one foot. "C'mon, answer the phone!"

After four rings, the call was answered. "Nick, are you watching *Sports Center*?" asked Luke.

"I was wondering when you'd call. *Sports Center*? You told me not to watch sports shows. You said something like they're *about* athletes and coaches, not *for* them."

"Yes, but, but, I was on *Sports Center* tonight."

"Oh, that's the reason for your excitement."

"To a fifty-five-year-old athlete, that is exciting. I was on for three or four seconds."

"Wow, a whole three or four seconds. Did you win the senior division or something?"

"No, and it's called masters, not seniors. They showed me going up Heartbreak Hill." Luke took a breather. "I guess I am being like a kid about this, aren't I?"

"Hey, you should be proud. I don't think I could run a marathon."

"I bet you could."

"I'll stick to just running around the bases. So anyway, what did you think of the game today?"

"I didn't see the game. How did you do?"

"I thought you watched *Sports Center*."

"I just turned it on. I missed the first fifteen minutes."

"What kind of personal coach are you when you don't know how I played today?"

"I'm sorry. I finished the marathon, talked with a few people, and crashed at the hotel, and then -"

"I hit four dingers."

Silence. Luke's eyes widened. He grasped for something to say and nervously laughed. "You hit four home runs on Patriots Day?"

"Yep. Three over the Monster and one to straightaway center. That one was a beauty."

"Holy crap!"

"Yeah, *Sports Center* did a funny little clip. They said in honor of Patriots Day in Boston, they showed me hitting the dingers to some famous classical tune. You'd know it. Every time the cannons went off, they showed me hitting the ball."

Silence. Luke shook his head in disbelief.

"They showed your highlights while playing Tchaikovsky's '1812 Overture'? That is awesome!"

"Yeah, I'd thought you get off on that."

"Let me tell you, Tchaikovsky is one of the greatest nineteenth century composers. While some may argue that the '1812 Overture' was not his most impressive work, with respect to recognition, it certainly ranks at the top. Did you know that it was actually the Boston Pops that began playing the '1812 Overture' as part of a Fourth of July celebration? So the ESPN writers were being very creative with this. Tchaikovsky's music can stir the soul, and talk about creative, he -"

"Luke, VT! That's great, but I really don't care. It's all I can do to listen to your man Bach while watching video."

"Sounds like its working. And don't try to tell me it's difficult to listen to. I'm sure you don't consciously notice it. It's there in the background providing audio support for your thoughts." Luke paused. "Hey wait a minute. How did you know about your *Sports Center* highlights? I thought you didn't see it."

"I watched the first ten minutes. Couldn't resist."

The broadcast studio was smaller than Nick had envisioned. Even the office building was unimpressive, nothing fancy or spectacular, a two-story building off Route 128 west of Boston. Nevertheless, Nick was nervous sitting next to the radio personalities. He noticed how comfortable they were, and in total command of their surroundings.

"You are dialed into the Joe and Bo Radio Morning Show," said radio host Joe Luther. "We're pleased this morning to have Red Sox third baseman Nick Hudson with us. For those of you who have lived in cave the first couple months of this season, Nick is the hottest hitter in the

American League and is a big reason why the Sox are in first place in the Eastern Division. Nick, welcome."

"Thanks guys, it's great to be here," Nick said.

"Nick, I think all of New England wants to know, what the heck has gotten into you?" asked co-host Bo Jamison.

Joe and Bo were radio show icons in New England. Their program centered on two major topics: New England sports and rock n' roll music. Their self proclaimed rock n' jock format was the top-rated morning show in Boston for their targeted audience – New England sports enthusiasts, age thirty and older.

Four years earlier, they ended their syndicated radio show on FM radio stations to enjoy greater opportunities on satellite radio, or as Bo said, "A license to cuss."

Their former act was racy and raunchy, with only a small portion spent on sports, and they did not play music. The previous show included satirical reviews of X-rated movies, skits with phone sex operators, and interviewing Boston area coeds, whose identities remained anonymous, to discuss the seedy aspects of college partying. The show's staple act was having listeners call for advice on how to deal with their problems – mostly marital, relationships, and sexual.

Joe and Bo, both in their late forties, recognized the radio business was changing because of satellite. They viewed this as an opportunity to produce a new format. Bo admitted, "It's been fun, but we want a new gig, a new challenge." Focusing on their passions of sports and music, the two entertainers created a show appealing to sports fans, with music from current and classic rock n' roll artists. Having established significant name recognition and a track record for success, they struck a lucrative deal with a satellite radio provider.

Their new show was labeled parental guidance by the entertainment industry, with occasional sexual innuendo and off-color remarks. Initially, Joe and Bo launched frequent obscenities, but the backlash was strong, as many parents listened with their children, and threatened to stop if the two did not clean up their act. They realized the cussing and crude comments added nothing to the show and were not necessary. And the music they played spanned generations. As Joe liked to say, "Regardless of age, our DNA embraces quality rock." Their focused strategy paid off; monetarily, professionally, and personally.

"I guess you could say I'm seeing the ball real well," Nick said.

"Yeah, you could say that!" exclaimed Joe. "Hey Stat Brat, what's our man Nick hitting now, what's his average?" Joe asked a young colleague who provided statistical information, production assistance, and someone for Joe and Bo to regularly tease.

"What's that?" Joe asked. "You say on-base plus slugging percentage is the more important stat. I want to know his batting average... I don't care if you're a card-carrying member of the Society for American Baseball Research, just tell us what he's hitting!"

"Four twenty-four! That's obscene!" Bo shouted.

"Okay Nick, it's time to come clean. It's what athletes do on our show. It's okay to cry, although we haven't had anyone do that yet. Let's go down the list," Joe said.

"Roids?" asked Joe.

"No."

"Amphetamines?"

"No."

"Other performance-enhancing drugs?"

"Nope."

"Corked bats?"

"Nope."

"Blood doping?"

"Not even sure what that is, so I can't being doing it."

"Juiced balls?"

"Hey! You can't ask that!" Bo exclaimed.

"I was talking about the baseballs, moron."

"Well, if that was the case, the whole league would be hitting like crazy," Bo said.

"All right, Nick, tell us how you've improved," Joe asked.

"Well, it's a lot of little things really. I can't say it's just one thing. I can summarize it best by a term I read from a book recently. I've become a servo mechanism."

"A what?"

"I've taken an approach where I've become, or striving at least, to be machine-like. But an excited machine. What I mean is, I really get into what I'm doing, but my approach is consistent, unwavering... a machine."

"Oh, I see, well you certainly are a hitting machine."

"Nick, we've heard you have an interesting diet. Can you tell us about that?"

"Yes. I pretty much drink protein shakes. I have grilled or baked fish with steamed vegetables three times per week. I eat lots of raw almonds too. I've learned that I need to consume foods that are good for the brain. With respect to my diet, foods that are good for the brain are good for the entire body. A friend of mine calls them brain brilliant foods."

"What do your teammates think of your diet?"

"They're cool with it. When you're playing well, you let the guy keep doing what he's doing."

"I guess so. Man, if I was performing like you I wouldn't change my underwear," Bo said.

"Bo, for my sake and our production staff, we'd want you to change your underwear."

Nick leaned back and laughed. Bo gave Nick a thumbs-up sign.

Joe then said, "All right everyone, we'll talk more with Nick Hudson. Right now we've got Aerosmith at the plate, Linkin Park on deck, and AC/DC in the hole. Later, we'll take calls on the Celtics and Bruins. Man, is late May a great time of the year or what. Celtics and Bruins in the playoffs, Red Sox playing awesome. You're listening to the Joe and Bo Radio Morning Show."

Bottom of the 5th

The trendy coffee shop on Newbury Street in Boston just completed their morning rush. Luke sat at a small, round table and surveyed the seating area. Tables to his left and right were empty. The counter service was busy and several customers sat on benches outside. He faced the front entrance, waiting for his appointment to arrive. Two cups of coffee and a black case lay on the table. Luke relaxed in his chair and smelled the coffee aromas. He noted the shop's stereo system needed to be adjusted for a clearer and truer sound.

A young man entered the coffeehouse, mumbling on his smart phone. He wore a black beret, thick-framed eyeglasses, modeled a ponytail, and a silver earring dangled from his left ear. The man carried a brown leather satchel. Luke glanced at him, and then checked the time on his watch. The young man stood at the counter for a few seconds. He then walked backward toward Luke's table while holding the smart phone to his ear, looking up at the shop's menu. The man pivoted on his left foot and plopped his body into the chair across from Luke.

"Gotcha," Nick said.

"Jeepers, Nick, what's with the, the look?"

"Quiet, don't say my name," whispered Nick.

"Is this your new off-the-field image? I kind of like it. You been hanging around my alma mater?"

Luke grasped the smart phone attached to his belt. "I've got to get a picture of this. My PCing friends will get a hoot out of this get-up."

"Calm down. I'm dressed this way because I have to. I could use your help, as a matter of fact. And for the record, like the earring, the hair's a clip on."

"Thanks for the clarification. So what's going on?"

"Have you been paying attention to the sports scene? It's out of control."

"Oh, you mean about your mug being plastered on every magazine and on sports shows."

"Yeah, I can't -"

"Do you know you didn't even suffer from the *SI* cover jinx? And your *Sporting News* cover, I dropped a few bucks and bought that one myself."

"Listen, are you my personal coach or personal fan? I need your help."

"Talk to me. By the way, that coffee is for you."

Nick glanced at the cup. "Coffee? I can drink coffee?"

"It's not on the bad list. As long as you don't drink sissy coffee."

"Sissy coffee?"

"You know, no cream and sugar, no whip cream, no flavored shots. Coffee has some health benefits. I drink four cups a week. So what help do you need?"

"Wow, four cups per week. You're out of control."

Nick raised the cup. He held it to his face, inhaled, and took a slow, lasting sip. He placed the drink back on the table and clasped the cup with both hands. He sighed and said in a low tone, "Damn, you could've told me about this earlier."

Luke and Nick were silent for a minute, sipping their coffee.

Luke restarted the conversation. "Your performance last night was solid. The ball you hit in the fifth inning was -"

Nick reached into his satchel and put a check on the table. "Here, I broke training last week. I made the check out to Luke Kelly. I assume that's okay."

"What happened?"

"I went home last Sunday night and Monday. Went to my favorite tourist shack on The Pier and wolfed down a dozen clam cakes. Washed them down with a twenty-ounce Coke. Man, those were good."

Luke glared and frowned at Nick.

"Oh, and later on, I had boiled lobster."

"With melted butter?"

"Of course."

Luke grimaced. "Jeepers, that's not clean, I hope -"

"By the way, don't you think five hundred bucks is a little steep?"

"Please, c'mon. You make about a thousand times that. That's my rule, the weekly fine is roughly your annual salary divided by a thousand."

"I guess that's fair."

"Well, I'm sorry you broke training. But my local Saint Vincent's de Paul Society for the poor thanks you for your donation." Luke snatched the check and stuffed it into his pants pocket.

Nick opened his satchel again, pulled out a baseball, and handed it to Luke. "This is for you."

"Thanks, that's nice of you." Luke inspected the ball.

"Do you know what's special about that baseball?"

"It's a Major League ball."

"True. It has the authenticity hologram and the commissioner's special stamp. And that's the ball I hit extending my hitting streak to forty games, a club record."

Luke's eyes widened. He glanced at the ball and back at Nick.

"I can't accept this. You should keep it."

"It's a gift, take it."

"No really, I can't... Wait a minute. I know just the place for this ball. There's a museum up the road from me, they'll be thrilled to display it."

"A museum? What -"

"Hey, let me show you something."

Luke placed the ball on the table. He grabbed his black case and pulled out a laptop computer.

"Not more protein shake recipes I hope," Nick said.

"No. This is really interesting."

"Baroque's greatest hits? Your situation silence journal? A surefire process to building a winning fantasy football team? I'm not betting it's your porn collection; you don't seem the type."

With a few keyboard strokes, Luke brought up a spreadsheet loaded with columns, rows, numbers, calculations, percentages, decimal points, abbreviations, acronyms, and colors.

"Look at this," Luke said, pointing to an entry on the busy spreadsheet. Nick stared at the screen and did not recognize the data, except for a few abbreviations.

"When I play my seven-string Ibanez, you're hitting over four hundred against right-handed pitchers at Fenway."

Nick said nothing and peered at Luke through his non-prescription glasses.

"And you clearly hit better with the Gibson when facing left-handed pitching. Now you're slugging percentage with the Fender is below average, but the on-base percentage at away games is strong. Check out -"

"What the hell are you talking about?"

"Isn't this fascinating? Depending upon which guitar I'm playing during certain game conditions, look what happens."

"You watch my games while playing the guitar? And keep stats on this shit?"

"Yes, I'd like to think I'm contributing."

Nick chuckled. "Have you lost it? Now I know what you meant when you described yourself as a borderline neurotic yet intelligent fan. You realize your guitar playing has nothing to do with my performance."

Luke sighed heavily and looked down at the keyboard.

"My God, you look like an eight-year-old who was just told there's no such thing as Santa Claus."

"I'm just having fun. For me it's a right-brain/left-brain exercise. I watch something interesting while practicing something I enjoy, and record the stats to keep my analytical side satisfied."

"Well, I feel better, but you need to get a life."

"There's nothing wrong with making practice interesting. And my guitar playing is therapeutic."

Nick scanned the coffee shop and checked his watch.

"You need to be somewhere?" asked Luke.

Nick ignored the question. "Why don't you go to a game?"

"I am serious, or rather superstitious about that. I use to go to plenty of games. I haven't been to a game in five years. I went to six games five years ago, and you guys lost all six. I vowed never to go back, for the sake of the team."

"C'mon, I wasn't even there five years ago. You should go to a game. Listen, we're playing the Yankees in a couple of weeks on the fourth of July in New York. I'll set you up with a ticket. Have you ever been to Yankee Stadium?"

"No."

"It's awesome. You gotta go."

"All right, I'll think about it. You said you need my help with something. What is it?"

Nick leaned toward the table and murmured, "The press is killing me. They're closing in on me. The clubhouse is like a friggin' circus after the game. Did you know about the Boston sports reporter who actually followed me to see if I was doing something illegal or against league rules?"

"No, you didn't say anything. Is it still going on?"

"No, not that I'm aware of. The skip had me report it to the front office and I guess it got taken care of."

"Let me know if that happens again. PCing has contacts who could help."

Nick laughed quietly. "What, PCing has a leg-breaking division?"

"No, let's just say PCing is well connected."

"Thanks. So do you have any suggestions for dealing with the press?"

"Gosh, I feel badly. I should have been more proactive about this. I do have some information and lessons to share."

"Don't feel bad. Lay it on me. By the way, this is a decent problem to have, isn't it?"

"Depends. You never know, things can go south real fast."

Luke raised his eyebrows, grinned, and held up his right index finger. He rotated the laptop toward him and pounded the keys.

"I've seen that look in your eye before. That creative process is churning. I can see it."

"Give me a minute," Luke said while typing. "Finish your coffee and we'll get into this."

Using a drawing program, Luke created a baseball infield. He labeled first base HONESTY. At second base he wrote HUMILITY. Typed HUMOR at third base. At home plate, he placed the word HIDE.

Luke turned the laptop so both could view the diagram. "I've adapted an informative lesson to share with you about talking with the press. Let's call it the four H's for effective communications with the press. The baseball field is for your benefit."

"This isn't some bad 'who's on first' joke, is it?"

"I think you'll find this helpful," Luke continued. "Let's say the bases are loaded and there's one out. A force at every base, right? You're the pitcher, the center of attention. If a ground ball is hit to you, where do you go with it?"

"That depends. Depending where it's hit, the score and the inning, and who's running, I could go to any of the bases."

"That's right, there's no set answer because of the variables. There may be several options that are good, and perhaps one or two that could be costly."

"We know, almost instinctual, where we're going with the ball if it comes our way."

"Exactly. You use your knowledge, experience, and anticipate how the situation will unfold. I see how quick you guys are. Most of the time when the ball is hit to you, you know right away what to do with it based upon the situation. Dealing with the press is the same thing. You have lots of options with your responses, but depending upon the question and the circumstances, most likely there are good and bad choices with respect to your approach."

"Okay, I see what you mean. You have honesty, humility, humor, and hide. I understand the first three, what do you mean by hide? Physically hide from the press?" Nick asked with a grin.

"No. In this example, I'm assuming physically avoiding the press is not an option. What I am talking about is not disclosing the information, hide it from them. Hide it because it's none of their business, it may be an inappropriate question, or it's information that if you divulged could cause problems for you or the team."

"You just described about all the types of questions I get lately."

"But let's go back to the other three. Take honesty. It's at first for a reason. Because it's the first thing you should think of. Honesty in this diagram is like a straightforward answer or response. It may not be glitzy or glamorous, maybe a boring answer, but it's a safe play... most of the time. Humility can be a favorable response. You guys use that one a lot. 'Aw shucks, I was just trying to make contact and the ball went out of the park.' But use too much humility and people won't see you as sincere. And humor, I would use that one sparingly. When the time is right, go for it. But be careful, it can backfire on you. In my baseball example here, there are not many times you would throw over to third base. Right?"

"Makes sense."

"Remember this: Think of questions from the press as if they were being asked by the opposing team's pitching coach... your competition. That should be your methodology. I'm sure you would be very careful what you would tell that coach if he were asking you questions. So be generic if you must, and don't give away secrets. And avoid saying 'no comment.' 'No comment' sounds like you're hiding something. Which you may be, but it's not a good response. There's plenty of broad responses you can give. Finally, you should practice some of your responses. Prepare for a television interview using a mirror."

"Sounds like brain burn. I like your little drawing," Nick said, pointing to the computer screen. "Guess that's why they call it fielding questions."

"The press is part of the culture and contributions to your profession. You need to keep that in mind. Respect them and they will respect you. You have good looks, a decent voice, and are intelligent. The media could help your career."

Luke heard a buzz at the coffee shop counter. Four teenage girls were bantering and giggling. Three middle-aged men stood by the door chattering, all looking at Nick.

"Sorry to say this, Nick, but I think you've been made. You better get out of here. Jeepers, you know you're making it big when teenage girls and middle-aged men are ogling you."

Luke and Nick gathered their things. Nick stood up and shook Luke's hand. "It was good seeing you, and see you in New York."

Top of the 6th

"Hot dogs, sausage, beer, pizza, popcorn, roasted peanuts. How do season ticket holders not become obese?" Luke thought as he scanned the stadium. "On second thought, maybe season ticket holders are obese," he wisecracked to himself after observing several overweight fans. Luke watched the Yankees take the field from his third base side box seat. Under his classic Boston ball cap, he wore a headset, tuned in to the Red Sox broadcast.

"Fourth of July, beautiful weather, Red Sox and Yankees at jam-packed Yankee Stadium. What kind of fireworks will we have today?" said the broadcaster. "Of course, it was Nick Hudson providing the burst last night, with two opposite field home runs, in the Red Sox nine–to–three victory."

"It's amazing, as we head towards the All-Star break, that Nick Hudson is halfway home to a Triple Crown," added the color commentator.

Luke reflected how much time had elapsed since he attended a Major League game. He admitted, Nick was right about Yankee Stadium, and although he sat among Yankee fans, the atmosphere was entertaining and exciting. He pondered what his PCing colleagues would say on the next conference call. "In my dreams, Nick's performance wasn't this good," he mused.

Luke took off the headset and took in the game, including all the senses that made being there in person so enjoyable. He chatted with the fans next to him, and participated in the good-natured, back-and-forth ribbing.

In the fifth inning, a young chubby man sitting to his right asked him, "Aren't you gonna have a beer or a dog or anything? If you're one of those health nut guys, they have organic hot dogs, you know."

Luke smiled at the portly fan. "Organic hot dogs? That seems like an oxymoron with respect to health food, but I'll take your word for it. Thanks, I'll pass. If I'm going to be bad, I'll go all-out, preservatives and all." Luke was not certain, but he believed the man mumbled "Weirdo" at the conclusion of their brief conversation.

In the bottom of the eighth inning, with the score tied at two, the Yankees were threatening to pull ahead with a runner on first and no one out. Luke, focused on the action of the game, put the headset on and listened to the broadcast.

"Alonzo Brown has a sizeable lead at first... The pitch from Evans... Cruz hits a flare into center that will fall in for a hit. Brown is rounding second and racing for third. The throw from Colby gets away from Hudson. Brown is safe at third. Hudson is down. We need to see this again. Colby's throw appears to have hit Brown's helmet as he was sliding into the bag and ricocheted into Nick Hudson. Brown remains at third, Evans was backing up third base and had to retrieve the ball."

"Nick Hudson is down and in pain. Brown is all right. Colby threw a BB and it skipped right off Brown's helmet. Let's watch the replay and follow the ball. You can see, oh my goodness, that's not a replay to watch if you're squeamish. Hudson takes the ball in the right eye. And he's still face-down with the training staff tending to him," said the color commentator.

"This has been an exciting game and enthusiastic crowd, but a sold-out Yankee Stadium is eerily silent right now," said the play-by-play broadcaster.

Luke, standing in front of his seat, felt his heart pounding. His face and neck flushed. He strained to see Nick, who was surrounded by teammates. He was relieved when Nick stood up - and sickened when Nick walked off the field into the dugout holding a blood-stained towel over his right eye, the team's trainer at his side. The packed stadium applauded, but

Luke heard nothing, his keen senses garbled from witnessing Nick's freak injury.

"Hey buddy," said the young man standing next to Luke, "you don't look so good. Don't like the sight of blood?"

"What? No, as a matter of fact I don't. Thanks for asking. I need to regain my composure. Nice talking with you today, good luck. I have to go."

"You're not gonna stay to the end of the game?"

Luke sighed heavily. "No." He adjusted his headset so he could hear any news about Nick, shuffled past the spectators in his row, and headed toward a stadium exit.

"What do you mean you weren't able to get through to him?" questioned a PCing member.

In his tenure with PCing, Luke had only participated in one other emergency conference call, and it was not his project. Only a project in crisis received this attention and response. Having less than twenty-four hours' notice, Luke felt vulnerable – naked. The preparation guru sat at the desk in his study with neatly organized notes and files, yet considered himself ill-prepared.

"Forget about that for a minute," interjected a colleague. "I think we need more robust dialogue regarding Luke's project, and I'm happy to start. First, several of us warned the group that something like this could happen. The time and resources spent may very well be for naught, with no, zero return on investment. I certainly didn't run my business that way. Second, why should we be funding projects with such high risk and minimal group knowledge about the industry? And it appears to me, a project based more upon one's personal interest. Finally, where's the contingency plan? There is no -"

"Hold on, everyone," said John.

The group was silent for several seconds. John chuckled. "Ladies and gentlemen, I know we're having a spirited meeting when all I see from Luke's video image is his... middle finger."

The group laughed, except for Luke.

"Luke, go ahead and take the floor. We've certainly barraged you this morning with comments," John said.

Luke leaned back in his executive black leather chair. He felt the rant building inside him. His palms sweaty, muscles tense. He took a deep breath and decided upon a different tack. Luke paused for effect.

"You know, we've been on this call for about ten minutes now. And none of you have asked how the student is doing."

The personal coaches said nothing. Luke observed a variety of expressions — raised eyebrows, dropped heads, frowns, and nodding in agreement.

"Excellent point," John said. "Thank you for the reality check and where our focus should have started. Please continue."

"Obviously, the media coverage about this has been huge, and you probably have seen the video, interview, and pictures. His right eye is rather grotesque. Totally red, watery, swollen. The good news, you may have heard, is that it's not his eye. He fractured his cheek bone."

"Can he play again this year?" asked a PCing colleague.

"I can't say. I mean I do not know, and neither does he. I was only able to speak with him briefly. Initially, I couldn't reach him at all, that's understandable. He's dejected, but I also sensed a glimmer of perseverance and resiliency. It's an interesting trait about successful athletes, something that's casually noticed but not truly appreciated."

"Let me ask, and by the way, are we still using the codename Hedgehog? John, anyone breaching this conference could figure out who the student is based upon what we are discussing," said a group member.

"It's okay. Use the codename per standard procedure. We are managing the risk," John replied.

The PCing member resumed. "How is the aura between you and Hedgehog?"

Luke rubbed his chin and curled his lower lip. "Interesting question, thanks for asking. I think it's excellent. I can feel it. He can be a real wise guy and he has a certain edge, but a solid teacher-student relationship exists."

"Thank you. Let me engage in some more robust dialogue. Why are we second-guessing our colleague at this point in the project's life? He has been successful to date, the project's status is still open, and according to Luke, we have a healthy student-teacher relationship. We all agreed this was high-risk and high-reward. And the monetary investment in comparison to other projects has been minimal. I recommend we hold off any decision about terminating the project until we know more about Hedgehog's ability to perform."

"I agree," said Hogan. "Seems like a few of you are in a... foul mood. Hey Luke, you like that one?"

The group members groaned and chuckled.

"Damn it, Hogan. Ladies and gents, yes we have experienced a setback. But you must admit his performance in Phase Two is nothing short of spectacular. I will be meeting with the student next week. I am confident I can keep the project progressing. Let me start Phase Three and we can reassess."

Luke prevailed. The PCing members approved his next step. Prior to ending the video conference, John addressed Luke and the group. "Luke, your salesmanship has pulled you through. But we have had more than a setback. Your project and group participation hangs in the balance. We all personally support you. Do not confuse challenges and concerns as personal attacks. We expect results. With your student's injury, your odds for success just got tougher. Let me speak your language. Amplify persistence and tone down optimism if you want sound results."

Luke sipped a tall glass of ice water. He noted the temperature was surprisingly tolerable for a Florida night in July. From an apartment unit below, Luke heard faint jazz music.

"I have to admit, your place is cleaner and neater than I expected," said Luke, sitting comfortably in a chair on Nick's apartment balcony.

Nick walked from the living room onto the balcony, holding a glass of ice water. "You can thank my mother. She's in charge of this place while

I'm gone. Wish I wasn't here, but, you know." Nick sat at the patio table across from Luke.

Luke peered at Nick's injured right eye and cheek. "Your eye looks a little better."

"Yeah, but not good enough. At least for a while."

"I read they put you on the sixty-day disabled list. Think you'll be able to play in September?"

"I hope so. Problem is, I can't do any minor league rehab if my return date is mid- or late September."

"I have to ask. What did you feel when it happened?"

"Luke, the ball was on me in an instant. I was hanging in there for the throw because I thought we had him. The pain was immediate. Things were dark. I never lost consciousness, but that would have been all right, considering the pain. Lying there face down, I just prayed that when I opened my eye, gunk doesn't come flowing out. Broken cheek bone, better than severe damage to my eye."

"I guess you were fortunate."

Nick sneered at Luke. "Yeah, if you call this fortunate. I certainly got my All-Star break."

Both men were silent for a minute. They drank their ice water to light jazz and the steady hum from a ceiling fan.

"I guess I really screwed up, huh?" Nick said.

"What do you mean?"

"No All-Star Game, no league-leading titles, should have taken the deal the team offered me last month, and screwed up your project."

Luke edged his body closer to the table. "Screwed up my project? Not so, it's very much alive. There's still a lot we need to do, and we will do."

"Isn't your project over? Your project, experiment, whatever it is, you could say it worked. At least for half a season. Go back to the league or players' union and report out, you know, whatever you're assigned to do."

Luke leaned back in the chair and crossed his arms. "You're on pain medication, aren't you?"

"I've enjoyed working with you. You're a smart guy, a little strange, but you're okay. I really appreciate all you've done. I did the things you asked me to do. Take credit for your teachings and ideas. There's probably a nice payday waiting for you."

Luke ran his hands over his brushed-back silver hair. "You think I'm working with you through the league or players' union?"

"Of course, why else would you be doing this? And how would you have access to the test I took last year? I'm not upset. Absolutely glad I did it and cooperated. I thought about going to the union rep about you, but I figured why spoil it since you said keep it confidential."

Luke's eyes widened and he muttered, "Talk about a pickle."

"Huh?"

"Nothing." Luke gulped down the ice water. He utilized the long drink to decide upon an approach.

"The season is far from over. We are going to keep working together. You're only halfway done with the reading list. You must stay with the program. Yes, we will finish the project. That's what we must do. Even with your injury, you can do the things we have gone over. I expect you to be playing again in September. You'll be there, they expand the rosters. And Red Sox Nation will certainly want you back."

Nick nodded yes with a wry smile. "Shit, I figured that was what you were coming here to tell me anyway. But listen, no more attending games for you. You're oh-for-seven now with a dude on the DL. I want you to stick with your guitar playing."

Luke laughed. "Sure. Any requests?"

"Whatever it is you play, VT, whatever you play."

Bottom of the 6th

Post-it flip chart sheets covered the conference room walls. Each sheet was numbered in the upper right hand corner. A discussion topic was printed at the top and underlined. The handwriting was in all capital letters using a thick, black marker. Of the twenty posted flip chart sheets, half were filled with enumerated comments. The other ten were yet to be crammed with information, ideas, recommendations, and questions.

Books, magazines, two black markers, two yellow highlighters, a few pens and pencils, a laptop computer, and a tray containing notebook paper lay on a large rectangular table in the middle of the room. A square, cardboard box, large enough to hold several books, and sealed with masking tape, was placed at one end of the table.

The room was thoughtfully prepared; from the furniture arrangement to the lighting to the temperature, designed to be conducive for learning and intense dialogue. The environment encouraged frequent movement and action – standing, sitting, listening, lecturing, reciting, debating, and writing on the flip chart paper. Luke was in his element.

"I hear you," Nick said, sitting at the conference table, "most of us have heard that before. Yeah, I'm the CEO or president of Nick Hudson incorporated. Have to look out for my best interests."

Luke stood up from the table and walked to a flip chart paper adhered to the wall. "No, you're not getting what I'm talking about. And I do not mean chief executive officer when I say CEO."

With the black marker, Luke wrote "CAPITALISTIC ETHICAL OPERATOR."

"The CEO abbreviation is important. It invokes power, influence, importance, responsibility, and leadership. So I always want my students to think of themselves as a CEO, whether they're the chief executive officer or not."

Luke continued with his lesson. "A chief executive officer may not necessarily be a capitalistic ethical operator. A chief executive officer is a position. A capitalistic ethical operator is a way of living. And you better believe that chief executive officers want CEOs working for them. Show me a successful, honest, hardworking salesperson and I'll show you a CEO."

"Hmmm... honest salesperson, didn't know there was such a thing."

"C'mon Nick, that's not fair. A rainmaker is an organization's most valuable player."

"I think good salespeople are selfish egomaniacs."

"Oh really, like there aren't any of those in professional sports."

"Well —"

"And what's wrong with selfishness?"

Nick raised his eyebrows. "That doesn't sound like something Luke Kelly would say. You okay, those marker fumes getting to you?"

Luke walked to the end of the table.

"Let me show you what I mean."

He pulled the cardboard box toward him and ripped off the masking tape. Luke removed a stainless steel blender, two small canisters, one ripe banana, and one bottle of water, placing each item on the conference table.

"Great. This your way of saying it's lunchtime?"

"No. Pay attention, Hudster, you need to understand the concept."

Luke poured the water into the blender. "Water; it's critical to support life and is mostly what we are made of."

Luke grabbed a canister, opened it, and emptied the off-white powder into the blender. "Lean protein, the key ingredient. And where the meal gets its name. By itself, is not enough, and by itself is not sufficient for a healthy diet. The leaner the protein, the better. Protein is selfishness. We need it to survive. Without it, we all cease to exist."

"Damn it, I just want lunch, get to the –"

Luke picked up the banana. "Ah yes, the good carbohydrate. Gives the nutritional drink taste and balances the protein." Luke peeled the banana and held it over the blender.

"Is that a blender or a volcano? You look like you're making a sacrifice to the gods."

Luke continued without hesitation. "The fruit represents morality and ethics. Without the fruit, chaos reigns. If the body is properly trained, protein craves the good carbohydrate. And if the mind is educated, selfishness seeks decency." He dropped the banana into the blender.

"Holy shit, I thought this was something to down at breakfast, not a friggin' explanation about life."

Luke remained focused on the presentation. He raised the second canister over the blender. "Good fats, omega oils, life's riches. Notice that it is the smallest ingredient, only a tablespoon." Luke added the flaxseed oil. "We need the fat, but good fats, and only in a small amount. People who have done without understand this very well."

Luke placed the lid on the blender. "Okay, student, what's next?"

"Mix it up."

Luke nodded yes and pressed the liquefy button. Nothing happened.

"Not sure if this is a life lesson, but do you need power?" asked Nick, holding the blender's electrical cord.

Luke smiled sheepishly. "Can't hurt."

Nick plugged in the cord and the blender mixed the ingredients. Luke reached into the box and removed a clear plastic cup. He poured the shake into it. He held the cup with both hands at eye level and said, "Live your life like this diet... clean."

Nick rubbed his chin. "Are we having a religious experience here?"

Luke handed the drink to Nick.

"So, back to selfishness," Luke said. "It's natural to be selfish; we just need to blend it with morality and ethics. I want you to be successful, and that includes making a lot of money. You need to become a CEO, capitalistic ethical operator. Our country thrives on CEOs. Their work provides for others. Many times it's indirect, but nevertheless, CEOs have impact."

"So you want me to be rich. Drive around in expensive, sporty cars, nice houses, clothes, the works."

"Cars are overrated. So are yachts. So is jewelry. Don't get me wrong, luxury items are fine, especially if the item represents a true passion or personal interest. But remember, adult toys may satisfy momentarily but they won't produce happiness."

"Nice one, VT."

"A friend of mine says, and I love this quote because of the business I was in, 'Money doesn't change who you are, it amplifies who you are.' And by the way, you're already rich, and I'm not talking monetarily."

"Yeah, I hear what you're saying. And besides, I'm not interested in a yacht or a boat. As a kid, I worked on my grandfather's boat, a commercial fishing boat. I love the ocean as much as the next guy, just don't want to troll around in it."

"Interesting. Nick, in our country and culture, it's noble to be a CEO. CEOs are people at the top of their game, extremely competitive, top earners, and help others earn more money. CEOs stimulate an economy. All professional athletes should strive to be a CEO, so should entertainers, business owners, salespersons, executives, lawyers, and many others."

"You expect all those folks to be selfish?"

"This self-sacrificing stuff has major limitations. A true capitalist does not sacrifice bunt. Capitalistic ethical operators go for it. They are heroes."

"When you say heroes, I think of firefighters, cops, soldiers, paramedics, nurses. Dudes on the front line."

"You're right, those people can be heroes. Let me give you an analogy. Their work can be compared to world-class sprinters. When you watch a one hundred meter dash, you are awed by the speed and power. You stand next to a sprinter and are totally impressed by the physique, muscle on top of muscle. Inspiring. CEOs are like marathoners. Yes, you have an appreciation for what the marathoner is doing, but the race is not exactly thrilling. Heck, most people could run awhile too. Stand next to a marathoner and you'd say the guy needs to put on some weight."

"You know, my agent would really appreciate this lesson."

"You're darn right he would. Just remember the E for ethical. The good fruit is critical. And by the way, there is another level above the CEO. These people are superheroes."

"Who are they?"

"We'll get to those later."

Nick sipped the protein shake, his mind churning. "Hey Luke, before we get back to summer school, tell me about your wife. What happened? If you're okay with me asking?"

Luke took a seat at the table. "You mean how did she die?"

"Yes." Nick sat down across from Luke. "Not just how she died, where did you meet, how long were you married?"

Luke leaned back in the chair.

"Karen and I met at Berklee. She was a music therapy major. Played the piano. She worked with handicapped children. She was talented and had a nice voice. But she wasn't into formal performances. I couldn't even get her to sing at some of the gigs I had. And believe me, we could have used a good vocalist. We got married a year after we graduated. We were married for twenty-six years."

"Wow. She must have been a saint to put up with your anal ways for twenty-six years."

"Excuse me Nick, but I wasn't always what you're calling anal. It's called discipline and attention to detail, and both have to be learned. With respect to attention to detail, one of the written values in my company was 'success is in the detail.' As far as discipline, I evolved, reinvented myself. Any of this sounding familiar?"

"I got your point." Nick smiled. "Go on."

"It was exactly one week after I sold my business. It was supposed to be a very happy time for us."

"What happened?"

"Karen was out walking in our neighborhood, energy walking as we both called it. She liked to walk while listening to music. She was killed by a truck driver who lost control. He was having a heart attack, and eventually died too. By the time I got to the hospital, she was gone."

"Damn, that sucks. I'm sorry."

"From what I can tell, she never knew what hit her. That's sounds bad, but it's the truth. The truck plowed into a large oak tree with Karen between the two. A few days after her death, I visited the accident site. It was cleaned up, except for what I think was a spot of blood on the tree. I haven't been okay with the sight of blood since."

Nick stared at a flip chart sheet, unsure what to say. "I'm sorry Luke, I didn't mean for you to relive that."

"It's okay."

"For what it's worth, you're an excellent coach."

"Thank you, but my current record doesn't say that."

"I've had some great coaches and managers, but they didn't win. Believe me, good coaching is important, but circumstances play a major role too."

"Hey Hudster, we need to get back to work. You'll be playing again in three weeks. Thank God the dog days of August are almost over. Grab that book about..."

Top of the 7th

"Since Nick Hudson's injury on July 4th, the Red Sox have played just under five hundred baseball," said the ESPN baseball analyst. "This, from a team that was winning two out of every three games the first half of the season. Now, with fifteen games left in the regular season, Boston finds themselves two games behind the Yankees. And prior to Hudson's injury, their team batting average was two ninety-three, since then they're hitting a mediocre two sixty-five. So this will be a special night at Fenway with Nick Hudson's return to the lineup. Of course, the question is, can he produce similar, or anything close to like, the offensive juggernaut he was first part of the year?"

"Jeepers, you better believe it's special," Luke said, watching the show from his downtown Boston hotel room.

Luke departed the hotel and strolled along the Boston streets. He thought about his former sound system business. Luke walked past buildings in which he and technicians had worked. Memories flowed. Systems installed with pride.

At Kenmore Square, he arrived at his destination – a quaint smoothie shop. He greeted the lone employee behind the counter and scanned the menu.

"Hey Coach, over here."

Luke was surprised to see Nick. "I can't believe you got here before me. We've come a long way."

"Don't flatter us. I lucked out and found a good parking space," Nick said.

"It was a nice thought while it lasted. So, big night tonight; you ready?"

"Abso-friggin-lutely. What inspiring lesson do you have today?"

"Nothing planned. Look, I don't even have my laptop. I just thought we'd talk."

"You, just talk? Isn't that like Bach saying 'let's just jam'?"

"Nice one. Order me the strawberry something-or-other, and hold the honey."

Luke and Nick chatted for fifteen minutes. They discussed the division race, weather, Nick's recovery, and their respective schedules. But they were also quiet at times, both men comfortable being together and being silent, neither feeling the need for continuous conversation.

"Okay, so there's no lesson today, but tell me, where did you learn about the things you've taught? You couldn't have made up this stuff yourself. Or did you?" Nick asked.

"Was that a compliment or an insult?"

"I didn't mean –"

"Years ago, this student finally got ready, and teachers have been appearing ever since."

Nick rolled his eyes. He cupped his hands over his mouth and nose. He exhaled deeply. "Luke, I am your father, just give me a straight answer," Nick said in a bass tone, doing his best to impersonate Darth Vader.

Luke smiled. "Fair enough. Years ago, seriously, I was lucky to hear about a group called The Executive Committee. It's an international organization for chief executive officers and top executives. Very much geared for entrepreneurs. Here I was running my business, needing help, and knowing I was not performing to the best of my abilities. So I joined this group. It changed my life."

"How?"

"It wasn't a social or political group, strictly business, but of course, friendships were forged. The group met monthly for pretty much the entire day. It offered a confidential and unbiased forum for business executives. I was able to address and work through business issues with my fellow group members, and help them with their issues too. Plus, there were outstanding speakers, covering a broad range of topics. These speakers were world-class, inspiring, excellent teachers. Finance to marketing to human resources to personal development to coaching, some great lessons and tools. So to answer your question, some of the things I am teaching you came from these resource speakers. And some I made up myself."

"Are you still involved with this group?"

"After I sold my business, I became a chapter chairman. That was incredible. Honed my coaching skills. I learned even more, in some ways through osmosis, by associating with talented, smart people. A few years later, PCing recruited me."

"Got recruited. I know a thing or two about that."

"I know you do. And at the end of this season, I bet you'll find the hot stove league real interesting."

"That's right, time for me to be a CEO."

"A CEO and then some," Luke said.

Nick finished his smoothie and stood up. "Coach, I need to go. Hey, you're not going to the game are you?"

"Heck no, I'll be at Logan within the hour. I'll be watching the game at home. Who's pitching tonight?"

"Mike Kern, a lefthander. Guess you'll be playing the Gibson."

"Damn right, Hudster."

Bottom of the 7th

"While we have a pitching change," said the play-by-play announcer, "allow me to paint the picture. An entire season has come down to the last regular season game, Sox and Yankees tied with ninety-three wins. The victor today wins the division, the other goes home. The wild card spot already wrapped up by Cleveland. Reynolds, an eighteen-game winner, is coming in to face Garcia. The Red Sox started the inning with a seven-to-four lead, but New York has pushed across two runs to make it seven to six. So here we are in the bottom of the ninth, two outs, the bases loaded and everyone at Yankee Stadium is on their feet."

Luke was on his feet also. He stood on his sofa in the family room, shuffling to find the spot which could squelch the Yankees' rally. "Cripes, why can't we just win the game in a boring fashion? Jeepers, we were up by three with our closer."

"The Sox have made this interesting. It would've been nice to have had a boring three-up and three-down inning," said the color commentator.

"Didn't I just say that? Cripes, I could do your job!" Luke shouted.

"Reynolds is set. The pitch, a fastball outside. One and oh to Garcia."

"Should I go to the guitar? No, that only works when hitting. Damn, where is the spot?" Luke said.

"Fifty thousand plus on their feet, this place is going crazy," said the color commentator.

"Crazy? I'll show you crazy. A fifty-six-year-old man standing on his sofa, trying to find the right position to get this guy out. That's crazy!"

"Reynolds gets the sign. The pitch, and it's fouled back by Garcia. One and one the count."

"A good pitch to hit. Reynolds got away with one. Garcia would like to have that one back."

"Have back... I'd like to have a lot of things back. Too damn bad."

His spontaneous comment removed Luke from the moment. Why, he asked, does he care so much for something he cannot control? "What if I did not care?" he pondered. "I am an intelligent, rational man, why do I get into the hype of this sport, this situation, whose outcome is beyond anything I directly impact? Is it because caring may be the only action I have, not worrying, but passionately caring for the desired outcome. And perhaps, just maybe, there is a dimension where those who intensely root, hope, and pray the most determine the end result."

"The pitch from Reynolds. A line..."

Luke dove from the sofa, stretching to his left. His body hit the carpeted floor. He kept his head up to view the display.

"Hudson snared the ball! Hudson snared the ball! Hudson snared the ball! The Red Sox win! The Sox are going to the playoffs!" shouted the play-by-play broadcaster.

"An absolute rope by Garcia. Hudson leaps to his left, fully extended, and snares the ball to end the game. What a play by Hudson!"

"Yes!" Luke yelled, sprawled on the floor. "Aw, forget about who roots and hopes the most, it's all about making plays. Atta boy, Nick!"

Luke realized this morning's meeting with Nick would be brief. He stood alone in the grand ballroom at the booked Chicago luxury hotel – the only room he found available. A large mahogany door opened. Nick entered carrying a spiral notebook.

"Coach, how the hell are you?" Nick said.

The two men hugged.

"Nick, I really appreciate you suggesting we meet. But I know your focus must be on the White Sox."

"C'mon, you're good karma, so long as you don't go to the game."

Luke glanced at the notebook Nick held in his hand. "Did you come here actually ready to takes notes?"

"Yeah."

"Heart be still," Luke said, placing his hand over his chest.

"Listen, Coach, I don't have a lot of time. Just start the lesson."

"Seriously, your concentration must be on the American League Championship Series, not a lesson from me today."

"It's okay. We talked about this on the phone. As long as it's short, that's cool. You provide a nice distraction."

"A nice distraction? Just what every teacher wants to hear, I'm sure."

"Hey, I brought a damn notebook, what more do you want?"

"Good point."

Luke and Nick walked side-by-side through the ballroom. Luke pointed out various objects in the room – lighting fixtures, speakers, chairs, bottled water and soda cans on a table. He rattled off information about each item, naming the manufacturers.

"Luke, I'm mildly impressed with your knowledge about lights from General Electric, but what's your lesson?"

"My lesson today is, what's your personal brand?"

"Personal brand?"

"Another key quality about being a CEO is you need to have an identity. A recognizable, positive trait you are known for. That's what companies want to achieve through branding. In our economy, branding is critical."

"Being a good Major League ballplayer is not enough?"

"Well, no, not if you want to be a CEO. If you were an above average salesperson for the best company in an industry, that would not make you a CEO."

"Okay, so what's my brand?"

"I can provide some suggestions, but it's really up to you. Sometimes your brand may be labeled by others. That's a beautiful thing if done by customers, and of course it's complimentary."

"What's your brand? No wait, I know, you're Luke Kelly the anal-retentive sound system man."

"Actually, you're close. My company and I did develop a reputation as being engineering driven. That's how we branded our services. Quality branding can increase the perceived value of a product or service, and of significance to you, a professional athlete. But here's the key: you have to live up to it, so your brand better be part of your DNA."

"I hear you, but I'm not exactly the flashiest player in the league."

"Your brand does not have to be flashy or funny. Think about it, Nick, you could be branded as a reliable, resilient, intellectual, clutch, right-time right-place kind of guy... except for one mishap. Those are all positive traits, and all marketable."

"Hmmm, Nick Hudson the intellectual baseball player, now that'll take me places."

Luke chuckled. "You'd be surprised. You know, even my wife had a brand."

"Your wife? A brand? VT, I really don't want to learn anything kinky about your wife."

"Get your mind out of the gutter. Seriously, Karen used to say that the universe is made up of music. Not sure where she got the idea from, but it was her funny expression, and she owned it among friends and colleagues. Her whimsical theory made a cute person even cuter. Want to know the weird part about that?"

"I thought that was the weird part."

"A few years ago, I'm at a hoity-toity cocktail party and I mention this to some guy. You know, just small talk kind of stuff. Two ice waters and a half hour into his dissertation, he presses me into defining music at its purest form. Finally, I gave him the answer he was looking for, energy waves or strings."

"Yeah, so?"

"Turns out the guy was a world-renowned physicist. He told me that's exactly what makes up the universe, and he told me to research string theory. I thought he was making a joke, since I told him I played the guitar. Jeepers, I must have come across as an idiot."

Nick smiled. "Coach, I have to go, but this has been an extremely valuable lesson this morning."

"You got a lot out of personal branding?"

"No. Hearing that you came across as an idiot."

Luke shook his head. "Cripes, you didn't even take notes."

"I forgot to bring a pen."

Top of the 8th

"A happy Halloween to all, and tonight we will see what tricks or treats are in store for the Boston Red Sox and defending champion Washington Nationals," said the ESPN baseball analyst. "Game seven of the World Series at Fenway Park for all the goodies. It's been an interesting series, although no player stands out as a potential MVP. Could it be Washington's Diego Torres who has been solid out of the bullpen, recording three saves? Or perhaps Boston's Nick Hudson, although he's hitting a meager two hundred for the series, has six RBIs, including three in game one, without recording a hit. But that's the way this series has gone. One could say it's been quirky. Both teams manufacturing runs in unique ways, and mustering enough pitching and defense to get to this point."

"Quirky? Let me show you quirky," Luke said, dressed in gray sweat pants, a tattered blue T-shirt, and white crew socks. He lugged a thirty-pound, hundred-watt Mesa/Boogie amp into the family room. "The things I have to do to get this team to win. Cripes, if Karen was here to see this, she'd have a good laugh."

His three favorite electric guitars rested in floor stands, lined along the wall adjacent to the media display center, the guitars tuned for tonight's musical selections. Three chilled twenty-ounce bottles of water sat on an end table, each one nestled in a coaster. Luke checked his sports watch. He scanned the preparations in his family room. "Game time in less than an hour. The amp needs to be programmed. Other than that, I'm ready."

The doorbell rang.

"Who the hell could that be?"

Luke opened the front door.

"Trick or treat!" shouted four children wearing costumes.

"Holy crap!" he yelled. "Cripes, I forgot all about this." Luke stood still in the doorway. He ran his hands over his hair. The children's Halloween bags rustled with impatience.

"Be right back, kids."

Luke scurried to the kitchen. He scoured the pantry and muttered, "Damn holidays and their candy. Sugar consumption in this country is totally out of control. We've got a friggin' epidemic going on and nobody cares..."

Luke found a solution to his problem and scampered back to the children.

"Here you go, kids. This is a very good and special treat. You'll like this, and if you don't, please give them to your parents, who probably need them." Luke dropped a pouch of prune juice into each bag.

Luke placed a bowl of fruit on the porch. He hung a sign on the front door which read, "Happy Halloween. Take what you like. Eat healthy. Go Sox!" Having dealt with the mini-crisis, Luke resumed his pre-game activities and settled in for the performance.

"And the Washington Nationals remain one out away from repeating as world champions, with the Red Sox scrapping and clawing in the bottom of the ninth," said the play-by-play broadcaster.

With his seven-string Ibanez strapped to his body, Luke stood silent and exasperated before the wall-mounted display. Sheet music and guitar picks littered the floor; the three water bottles, empty. He looked up at the ceiling and sighed. Luke glanced at a decorative chest, with a southwestern design, in the corner of the room.

"Regardless of the outcome, what a series, what a game. Halloween, a crisp autumn night, game seven at a historic ballpark. You can't script this," said the color commentator.

"Torres, Washington's all-star closer, has his work cut out for him. Tony Gregory stands at second. The speedy Rooster Colby, who drew a two-out walk, is on first. Chris McGrane represents the tying run at the plate."

"C'mon, Chris, stay alive." Luke placed his guitar on the stand. He walked over to the chest and stared at it — memories churning in his mind.

"The pitch from Torres, McGrane hits a chopper down the third base line. Hernandez has to eat it! He's got no play!"

"A Baltimore chop hit by McGrane. Hernandez kept it from going into left, but there was no play for him. The bases are full."

"What a ninth inning this has been. The bases are loaded, two outs. Washington clings to a six-to-three lead. And Nick Hudson steps to the plate."

Luke knelt before the antique chest. He unlatched the clasp and opened the lid. "I know it's in here somewhere."

"Sox fans won't want to hear this, but Nick Hudson is oh-for-nine lifetime against Diego Torres."

"Torres was a great free agent acquisition by the Nationals to replenish their bullpen. Washington scooping up a quality closer from the Orioles, their American League rival."

Pushing away yearbooks, programs, books, magazines, and newspapers, Luke rummaged the chest until he reached the bottom. He grasped a book of sheet music with both hands. Luke read the handwritten note on the cover and grinned. "Use only in case of emergency, October 2004. Love, Karen," stated the note with a smiley face. Luke flipped through the book and found the song. "Heck, I even wrote down the amp settings."

"Home plate umpire Bruce Fuller breaks up the meeting on the mound," said the play-by-play announcer.

"A smart move by the Nationals to huddle. Remind everyone there's a force at every base. Go over defensive positioning. Settle down Torres."

"And did you notice a quick little smile on Nick Hudson's face as he stood outside the batter's box surveying the field?"

"He must like the spot he's in," said the color commentator.

Luke placed the book on a music stand. He adjusted the control knobs on the amp. He faced the media display and strummed the cherry red Ibanez, commencing the ballad.

"Here we go folks, two outs, bases loaded, bottom of the ninth, Nationals leading six to three. Everyone on their feet at Fenway. Hudson readies himself at the plate. The pitch from Torres. Whoa, a fastball up and in, and Hudson has to bail out."

"Ah yes, chin music from Torres."

"Chin music! I'll show you chin music!" Luke cranked the volume on the amp. He grabbed the remote control and activated closed captioning. Luke watched the pitch count rise. Nick battled Torres, fouling off pitch after pitch.

The shrieking sound waves bounced off the family room walls. Recalling the song, Luke played without viewing the sheet music. His vision focused on Nick's at-bat, his body absorbed with the music. He belted the lyrics and swayed his shoulders. His fingers glided across the instrument with confidence. The chords rang true. "Damn, this sounds good," he thought.

"The pitch from Torres... a deep drive to left!"

Luke stopped playing. His eyes widened.

"Way back, way back, it's gone! A grand slam home run by Nick Hudson! Red Sox win! Red Sox win! Red Sox are the world champions! Total pandemonium!"

Luke dropped to his knees, arms raised in triumph, the guitar strapped to his body.

"Hudson crushed the ball! It's Lansdowne bound! It may have hit the turnpike! Sox win seven to six!"

"This place is rocking!" shouted the play–by–play broadcaster.

Luke pumped his fist. "Yes!" He watched the players mob Nick when he landed on home plate. Luke's head throbbed from the excitement. "Nothing else matters, nothing else matters. Metallica still has game."

Bottom of the 8th

Luke rang the doorbell, holding the evening meal under his arm. Nick opened his apartment door. The two men stood still for several seconds. They stared at each other and grinned.

"Unbelievable," Nick said.

"Yes, I can't believe it either. A grand slam to win the World Series."

"No, I'm not talking about that. I can't believe you really did bring pizza and beer."

"You know Nick, you need to lighten up."

Luke and Nick enjoyed their celebratory dinner at the small kitchen table. A pre-Thanksgiving treat meal, they said. The two men joked about the nutritional values gained from beer and pepperoni pizza. After several minutes and two slices, Luke leaned back and shook his head. "I have to ask, what were you thinking when you smiled just before stepping into the batter's box?"

Nick finished his beer. "I've had a bunch of questions about that. I tell them I didn't even realize it, and it must have been my way of dealing with the pressure."

"I take it you're hiding something?"

"I can confide in you, right? I mean, this is kind of strange, but you're involved, involved big time."

"What, what were you thinking about?"

"You remember our trip to Cathedral Rock." Nick paused. "This is too weird, never mind."

"Go ahead, Nick. Of course I won't say anything."

"Well, when I was swinging the bat on top of the rock to the music, I pictured the whole thing."

"Hitting a home run?"

"No, I mean the whole damn thing. World Series, game seven, bases loaded, two outs, and get this, playing the Nationals with Torres pitching."

"Okay, that is strange."

"Abso-friggin-lutely. I knew Torres had signed with the Nationals. And I ended the season before by striking out against him. So I envisioned the entire event on top of the rock, because of your damn exercise. Before stepping into the batter's box, I remembered it. That's why I smiled. I just knew I was going to hit the ball hard. I could feel it. I felt incredibly confident."

"So, Hudster, still think it's mumbo jumbo?"

"I don't know, but I'm definitely going back. This time with my driver."

After two beers each and Nick eating the last pizza slice, Luke lobbed another question. "Can I share a couple of things with you? Things I think you should know about me and PCing."

"Oh no, here it comes. Is this the point I have to kick your ass? You're not going freaky on me now. Shit, two damn beers and you're probably wasted. I can only imagine what effect tonight's food must have had on your finely tuned system."

"Bite me, Hudster. I want to tell –"

"No, wait. Seriously. I want to share something with you first. To a teacher and coach, this feedback is important."

Luke smiled. "By all means. Please share."

Nick pointed to the empty pizza box and held up a Michelob Light beer bottle. "Take pizza and beer as an example. By themselves, they taste good. But together they taste great, they complement each other. That's what I got from your coaching and teaching. Situation silence, get an NBA, the reading, baroque music, protein shakes, the fines, brain burn, and practical prayer are good stuff. Those things work if you keep up with them. But they became great when we simply talked every week. Our weekly conversations and side lessons were a needed getaway. An educational retreat that I believe made my game sharper. It was very helpful for me to talk with someone on a regular basis who was outside the lines. And someone who didn't act like a giddy fan. You inspired me physically, intellectually, and emotionally. In a nutshell, that's what you brought to the table."

"Wow. I'm impressed. Nice touch with the visual and taste senses of the beer and pizza. Well done."

"Okay, so what do you want to share with me?" Nick asked.

"Turn over the pizza box."

"Huh?"

"Turn over the pizza box."

Nick flipped the box over. Taped to the back was an eight–inch–by–ten-inch color photograph.

"Who's the freak and the hot chick?" Nick asked.

"The hot chick is my deceased wife, Karen. The freak is me."

Nick's eyes widened. He snickered. "No way."

"Yes, Nick, that's me about thirty years ago."

Nick inspected the photograph, smiling. "Look at your long hair and beard. Tattoos? Earrings? Bracelets? Is that a necklace of smashed beer cans? Holy shit, are you wearing spandex?"

"Yes. I was the lead guitarist for a band called Sheet Metal. For some songs, I would get Karen to play the keyboard. That's a photo of us taken at a club in Boston."

Nick shook his head in disbelief. "Sheet Metal? Are you joking? Listen, I must say, you're a complex dude."

"And that's one of the things I wanted to share with you. There was nothing wrong with who I was then or my looks. But over time, I evolved. I wasn't a stick in the mud. My changes in appearance are only an expression of my ability to adapt, improve, and learn. I've had some people ask me if I found religion. I've always had religion. My religion told me, and was always telling me, to be more disciplined. My core was solid, defined. I just kept polishing it. That is what I want you to remember."

"I'll certainly remember this," Nick said, holding the photo. "Can you autograph this for me?"

The evening conversation continued for two hours. Luke reiterated several instructions and wrote key points on paper for Nick to keep. Numerous details were discussed and clarified. Luke relished the passionate dialogue. They shook hands when the plan was finalized.

"Cripes, it's eleven o'clock. I need to get going," Luke said.

"Listen, Coach, before you go." Nick hesitated. He searched for the right words, a profound statement. Nick chuckled at his inability to grasp a deep one-liner. "Thanks for everything, really."

"You're the one making it happen. You cooperated, listened, applied, and persisted."

"Yeah, I got the clap."

"Gosh, that sounds awful. I need to create a new acronym for my process."

"Yes, please do."

Luke walked to the door. He stopped and turned around. "Now remember, do not back down. Tell your agent what we have discussed. He may balk at first, but you're the friggin' man right now, so you call the shots."

"Yeah, I got that too. Hey, wait a minute. You told me about your heavy metal roots, my God I still can't believe it, but you never talked about PCing. Something I should know?"

"Oh yeah, well, we can get to that later. Focus on your plan for now."

Top of the 9th

Reporters gripped their digital audio recorders, waiting for the press conference to start. Television cameramen and photographers jostled for the best position and angles. The brightly lit media room buzzed with conversations. Video and audio equipment produced a low hum.

Wearing a gray Armani suit with burgundy tie, Nick strode to the head table on a small stage, the team's logo decorated backdrop behind him. Camera flashes clicked and burst toward Nick.

Nick sat upright in a chair, alone at the table; his agent and the team's general manager standing off to the side. He gazed at the throng of media personnel. "Good morning, everyone. First, let me say it's great to be here." Nick removed a paper from his suit jacket pocket and placed the paper on the table. "I want to get this right, so I wrote down a few statements and thoughts to share with you."

"How do you feel about your deal?" shouted a reporter.

"I'm very pleased."

Questions erupted simultaneously. Nick scanned the crowd. He located his longtime acquaintance, Pete Sullivan. Nick obliged his friend, ensuring his questions were heard. Sullivan was a colleague, a witness to Nick's accomplishments and losses since high school. They treated each other with respect. "Sully, go ahead."

"Because of your heroics in the World Series, how much impact did that have in getting such a lucrative contract?" asked Sullivan.

"A nicely timed hit certainly can't hurt," Nick said with a sly grin. He glanced at the paper. "Let me add, hitting a grand slam home run does not make me a hero. I've read and heard that term being said about me. Playing a professional sport gives me the opportunity to become a hero. Am I a role model? Yes. A hero? I'd like to be a hero, heck maybe even a superhero. But I have a lot of work to do to get there, and it's not exclusively about on-field performance."

Even with the blinding camera flashes and bright lights, Nick noticed several reporters smirk and frown.

Sullivan addressed Nick again. "Do you think that growing up in Rhode Island and playing college ball at Maine helped in the negotiations with the team?"

"Well, as my agent told me, a nicely framed background certainly can't hurt."

"What do you plan upon doing with your newfound wealth?" another reporter asked.

Nick paused and scanned the crowd. "I'm giving it all away."

Murmurs, laughter, and gasps spread across the room.

"You just signed a deal with the Red Sox that makes you one of the highest-paid players in the league, and you're giving it all away?" exclaimed a reporter in the front row.

"Yes I am. To clarify, I am donating my entire salary, and will continue to do so as long as I am playing Major League ball. I have established a foundation to provide donations to national, international, and local charities, especially local charities. And I have a couple of charities, or call them causes, that are dear to me, which I will strongly support. Listen, everyone, I really don't want to make a big deal about this. But you asked the question, so you got a straight answer."

"Why would you do this? What about your financial security?"

"I certainly care about my financial security. Along those lines, I am pleased to announce I will be endorsing products from three great companies. It would be inappropriate for me to mention the companies by name at this time, but you'll hear more about this soon. What I can share with you is this: The deals I have with these companies provide me with total financial security. I am a baseball player and a capitalist, and I am proud to be both."

The reporters blurted questions. They stopped when Nick resumed. He felt the heat from the lights become hotter.

"By the way, I would like to thank my agent for arranging meetings with the CEOs of the companies I am endorsing. We had very productive meetings. I believe in their products and the brand image they wish to create. I also support and agree with their overall business objectives, direction, community involvement, and management philosophies."

A reporter raised his hand. "With respect to some recent problems professional athletes have had with the law and their personal lives, did you have to sign a morality agreement with these companies?"

"Interesting question. Thanks for asking. Yes I did. And I also required the CEO to do the same. If the CEO breaks the terms of our agreement, I am free to terminate the contract and endorse a competitor, if I choose to." Nick chuckled. "As you can imagine that was a tough one to pull off."

"Hey Nick, does this make you baseball's version of Robin Hood?" shouted a reporter.

"Robin Hood? And my teammates a band of merry men? I don't think so." The reporters laughed. Nick pointed to a reporter for the next question. Before the reporter spoke, Nick continued. "Robin Hood stole from the rich and gave to the poor. I don't like that analogy. But how about this one: I will work with the affluent to help the needy. I must admit, my goal is to be a philanthropic capitalist, or PC for short."

"Do you think this will set a trend for other professional athletes?"

"I'm not doing this to set a trend. I'm doing this because I believe it's the right thing to do. If others choose to follow, that's fine. I'm reminded of a quote by Ralph Waldo Emerson, 'Do not go where the path may lead, go instead where there is no path and leave a trail.'"

"While you're doing this, um, PCing stuff, do you think that will affect your play on the field?"

"Excuse me," Nick said with a startled expression. "Did you say PCing?"

"Yes. Just using the verb tense of your abbreviation. So do you..."

Nick stared into the lights, his thoughts churning. He beamed. "Baseball with peak performance is my top priority. My focus will be on my business, and that's baseball."

The press conference lasted another ten minutes. The questions transitioned to off-season plans, his relationship with the team, and thoughts about achieving similar results for the upcoming season. Nick displayed poise fielding the inquiries. After Nick left the press conference, while driving to his Brookline apartment, he called Luke.

Bottom of the 9th

"I can't believe how bad you are at this game," Nick said. "Didn't you tell me you live on a golf course?"

Luke placed his mud-stained five-iron into the golf bag. "I've been thinking about getting lessons."

"You may want to think about giving it up. Golf isn't for everyone."

"Thanks for the motivation."

It was a slow day on the golf course. Two foursomes ahead dragged out the pace. But neither Luke nor Nick cared. At the end of nine holes, Nick was shooting par, and Luke stopped keeping score. They relaxed in their golf cart, waiting to tee off on the tenth hole.

"So, how's life?" Luke asked.

"Damn it, you and your questions. You're worse than the press."

"Okay fine, a simple question then, what are your plans for Christmas?"

"I'll be in Rhode Island with family and some friends."

"That's nice." Luke grabbed a box of golf balls from the front compartment. "So how's your love life?"

"Aw shit, Doctor Shrink has arrived. I knew it."

"I'm interested in –"

"How's yours, VT?"

"I'm seeing someone. Met her while jogging in the neighborhood. I live in a swinging community you know."

"Yeah right, maybe a swinging gate community."

"Nice one. So, what about you?"

"If you must know, I've hooked up with an old high school friend. Things are going well. And you'll appreciate this. She's a music teacher at a Catholic high school. I think she's more impressed with my knowledge of baroque music than anything I've done on the baseball field."

"That's great. How come you didn't tell me about this?"

"It's none of your damn business."

"C'mon, I'm your personal coach."

"Just grab your driver and hit the friggin' ball. Try not to hit a house this time."

Upon completing the golf round and putting away their clubs, Luke and Nick adjourned to the Sable Palm conference room. They reclined at the table, sipping ice water.

"Should I inform the country club it's now safe for children to play in their backyards?" Nick asked.

"Hey wise guy, do you want me to tell you about PCing or not?" replied Luke.

"Is this going to involve any of your famous audio-visual tools?"

"No, sorry."

"Thank God. Go ahead, I'm listening."

"I'm not sure where to start. Let me clear up something first. PCing was not in any way connected to the league or players' union."

"Yeah, I eventually figured that out. But who are you guys?"

"I'm sworn not to tell more than I am allowed. PCing is a wonderful group of caring people. There are a few common denominators about us. We are all multimillionaires, even a couple mega-millionaires. And all intellectuals. I'm talking Mensa-league talent. Most are far more intelligent than I. What I lack in smarts, I try to make up with persistence and creativity."

"I'll give you that, Mister Sheet Metal."

"There's another common denominator, but I cannot divulge that. More importantly, I need to tell you about your endorsement deals."

Glumness fell upon Nick's face. "What didn't you tell me?"

"Let's just say those CEOs you met with have been in your shoes."

"You coached them?"

"Not me, a PCing colleague. We can call him Abe."

"You sly dog, you stacked the deck."

"Stacked the deck? That sounds like I cheated. What I did was increase our odds. The project was laid out that way."

Nick chuckled. "I feel so used."

"Really?"

"No, I feel damn good. Of course I knew those CEOs were connected to PCing. Why else would you direct me to those specific companies? Plus, I could tell by the things they said, a little gleam in their eyes. It was business networking on a fraternal scale."

"Gosh, I am so proud. I could cry."

"You did enough of that on the golf course."

His house was peaceful, the study immaculate. A chilly and damp December afternoon kept the golfers home. Luke stared into the solid blue computer screen, waiting to access the conference.

"Welcome, Luke, we salute you," John said. The video images appeared on the screen. Each image showed a waving middle finger. Luke shook his head and chuckled.

"One indiscretion at one video conference and you won't let it go," Luke said.

"It wasn't an indiscretion, it was a video conference classic highlight," replied a PCing member.

"Just be happy I didn't moon you. Hogan, don't say a damn thing."

The group laughed.

"Okay, everyone, you've read Luke's report. There are a few announcements which –"

"John, before we go further, I have an announcement I would like to make," Hogan said.

"If Luke is okay with it."

"Sure, Hogan, please take the floor," Luke said.

"Well, even though Luke's project spanned a longer time period than usual, and it experienced a near collapse, I formally nominate it for PCing's project of the year."

PCing members applauded. "Luke, Luke, Luke," they chanted. Luke crossed his arms and sighed. He refrained from grinning.

"I second that," said another member.

"Ladies and gentlemen, Luke's nomination is noted. Luke has something to share with us, so please give him your attention," John said.

Luke sat up in the chair. He cleared his throat to address the group. "You will be pleased to hear I am wiring John a generous amount of money from the Hedgehog. He said he wanted to reimburse us for the project's costs and he added some to fund another project."

The group applauded and broke into the Luke chant again.

"All right, everyone, that's enough. We're not exactly businesslike today, are we?" John said. "Luke, please continue."

His face flushed and his ears reddened. Luke took a deep breath. "On a personal note, I have the honorable distinction of resigning from the group due to the complete and total success of my project." Luke paused. He heard and observed the stillness. "I am thrilled to announce I am launching a new career as the executive director for the Nick Hudson Giving It All Foundation."

The group members said nothing. Luke viewed the PCing associates' stares without expression.

"I knew I shouldn't have nominated him," Hogan said, breaking the silence.

For Luke, an awkward five minutes passed - filled with congratulatory remarks and accolades. Embarrassed and desiring a different subject, he interrupted, "Can I still attend the Christmas party?"

"Yeah, if you promise to play something," Hogan said.

"Of course I will. And I've added some strong material to my annual jingle jam."

"We look forward to your performance," John said.

After the meeting concluded, Luke sat back in his chair. Thoughts rambled in his head – his schedule, goals, the Foundation, and how Nick was doing. He looked out the window and saw a lone golfer teeing off in the raw weather. Luke walked to the family room. He picked up the remote and entered the channel.

"Welcome to Golf Channel's *Lessons for the Golfing Challenged,*" said the host.

"I will improve," Luke said. "I will improve."